FAIN
THE
SORCERER

Steve Aylett is the author of *Slaughtermatic,
LINT, The Complete Accomplice, Rebel at the End
of Time, Toxicology, The Inflatable Volunteer,
Atom, the Tao Te Jinx, The Crime Studio,
Bigot Hall, Shamanspace, And Your Point Is?,
Smithereens and Novahead.*

ALSO FROM SCAR GARDEN PRESS:

NOVAHEAD
THE COMPLETE ACCOMPLICE
SMITHEREENS

SCAR GARDEN Kindle editions include:
FAIN THE SORCERER
NOVAHEAD
SLAUGHTERMATIC
SHAMANSPACE
TOXICOLOGY
ATOM

FAIN
THE
SORCERER
STEVE AYLETT

INTRODUCTION BY ALAN MOORE

If we loved Steve Aylett, really loved him in the way that he deserves, a selfless love that genuinely wanted nothing save his happiness and comfort, we'd lobotomise him. Nothing complicated or too costly, just a well-judged swipe with shovel blade or flat iron when he isn't looking ought to do the trick. This would afford him satisfaction in more ways than one. Firstly, it would confirm his previous opinion of us personally and of humanity in general, and secondly it might impair him mentally, thus furthering his career. If he could just stop the Tourette's flood of original ideas, dilute the language so the reader only had to pause and shake their head in admiration every paragraph or so rather than every other line, this man could be a sales phenomenon, could be a franchise, it's all just a shovel-blow away. There would be glowing twelve-year-olds lined up in Waterstones at midnight for the latest Beerlight or Accomplice saga, there'd be blockbusters, Jeremy Paxman flirting openly with Aylett during *Newsnight*, Lint confectionery, Hell toys. Best of all, with his critical faculties all having gone the same way as his frontal lobe, he'll have no idea that he's writing tepid drivel and can just enjoy himself, can ride round Tunbridge Wells in a gold dodgem car, eating cream cakes and laughing.

Clearly, though, none of us love him that much, and especially not those of us who love his work. We'd prefer, for his sake, that he could be brilliant with a large, sophisticated audience whose polish was sufficient to reflect his dazzle but, in lieu of that, we'll settle for brilliant-and-suffering. There are few people who can suffer as amusingly, revealingly or fruitfully as Aylett can, nobody with a talent for the torment so that they can turn their horror at the ocean of stupidity around them into something at once visionary and disablingly funny. It should also be said that within the field of fantasy and science fiction there are very few creators half as dogged or uncompromising in the pursuit of their muse as is Steve Aylett, or with such good reason.

With the death of William Burroughs, J.G. Ballard mourned the passing of one of the last committed writers, noting that Burroughs' demise had left us only 'career novelists', the ones who had already lined up for the lucrative, blunt-spade accomplished neural surgery as mentioned earlier. These wordsmiths, spayed and tame, know where the grazing land is good and never wander past the stinging cattle-wire of audience comprehension out into the income-threatening wilderness beyond, out into the disreputable pulp-jungles of genre, into art. They know enough to hoard their fuel, dilute the energy to homeopathic doses that will not prove toxic to their audience or sales, to make one second-hand and borrowed concept last a chapter, last for a whole book. Whatever else you do, for God's sake don't burn twenty new ideas with every page as blazing throwaways. That just makes all the other workers on the line look bad, and anyway the constitutions of the readership are for the most part not adapted to ingest raw fire, preferring in the main its faintest after-taste, a water-memory of fire rather than the untreated magma.

Aylett, thankfully, has never met or listened to these

people, and instead is gloriously unaware which side his bread is buttered. He just keeps on hurtling along, a Porky Pig express train that's dismantling its own box cars to provide the sleepers for the tracks ahead as it roars smoking out amongst the cartoon cacti. When he first emerged in the science fiction field it was into a world of categories and labels that had no idea what to make of him. Was he a cyber-punk, a nano-punk, an Alfred Jarry pata-punk, or just somebody who'd turned up to take the piss? Was this science fiction comedy, in which case why no punning titles, why no obvious Robert Sheckley retreads, no easy referents, no 'in the grand tradition of...'? Why weren't there any plots that worked as a three-minute pitch, a three-line jacket blurb? Was he just trying to unsettle everyone?

In fact, Steve Aylett was no kind of literary punk at all. He just liked sunglasses, and that's what had us all confused. If there are any influences to be glimpsed in the almost self-conscious and relentless onslaught of sheer novelty that is his work, they seem to be the influences of an earlier time when there was nothing punk and not much outside *Dr. Who* was cyber; of a period where, when it came to science fiction authors, individual voices were appreciated, and were more than that, demanded. Had he not been born, with perfect Aylett irony, in the Summer of Love - been born too late - he might have had a Michael Moorcock *New Worlds* as a vehicle, have had a context in amongst all of the other brilliant, mismatched oddballs. Aylett is in many ways a staunch traditionalist in that he harks back, ultimately, to the Judith Merrill days when science fiction still had a tradition of originality, before we based our writings on a calculated demographic strategy, when intellectual shock was one of the main reasons that we bothered with science fiction in the first place, and when trilogies of sorcerer-infested fantasy were the exception rather than the norm.

Which brings us to this current volume, *Fain the Sorcerer*, concrete proof that had Steve Aylett launched himself into the marketplace of fantasy rather than that of science fiction, then he would have been no less a marvel nor a prodigy, and he still would have frightened and bewildered us by turn. This is not comic fantasy in the restricted sense the term is used today, the knowing and post-modern slapstick with the title that lampoons a work more widely known, but is instead aggressively inventive, with a comedy that's unrelenting, one of those transcendent satires that ends up a radiant, sublime example of the genre that it's satirising, like Polanski's *Fearless Vampire Hunters*. This is fresh, exciting comic fantasy, but it is also fresh exciting fantasy without the qualifier. Speaking as someone who for some years now has had difficulties with the concept of magical fantasy, this book was a reminder of the way that it was meant to work, a nitrous oxide rush of notions that at times recalls Jack Vance's *Dying Earth* as it might be hallucinated by an M.C. Escher, with its self-imperilled hero and the labyrinthine mess he brings upon himself more than a match for Vance's Cugel.

In fact, as is the case with Aylett's greatest influence, Jeff Lint, one can sense an oblique resemblance between the author and his subject. One gets the impression that what drew Steve Aylett to the understandably neglected Lint was simple kinship. Maybe Aylett too once had an agent that turned out to have been dead for years. This current book suggests at least an empathy between the author and what is in this case his entirely fictional creation, Fain the Sorcerer. Like Steve Aylett, we have a protagonist whose very ingenuity is his undoing, who has somehow found a scam whereby he can unreel a seemingly unending list of magical abilities which both bewilder and delight. At one point in the narrative Fain backs away dispensing gold coins from one pocket of his coat and sardines from the other, which is an illuminating metaphor for the entirety of Aylett's oeuvre.

Read the book, first to yourself, then, unavoidably, aloud to friends until they're sick of you. Hope that Steve Aylett's soul-destroying trail of tears continues if this is an indication of the nuggets that he's finding on the way. Hope also that he one day realises how ridiculous he is and is delivered in that instant to a lovely mask-faced mermaid, all his endlessly amusing tribulations done. This is a stunning work of the imagination that is also very, very funny, from one of the most exciting and innovative creators to emerge in years. See him, the fabulous self-cursing magus as he backs away, flinging his golden talents and his glittering sardines, each as enticing as the other, offering not only opulence but also salty nourishment. This book, replete with both, is an extravagant and satisfying feast that you should savour, even while resisting the temptation to devour it in a single sitting. Aylett is a jeweller, and this work is one of his most finely chiselled gems. Hold it up to the light and study at your leisure.

Alan Moore
Northampton
July, 2005

'It's pretty but it's very very heavy'
                                    —*Deathwhisker*
                        Anna Padgett (The Naysayer)

CHAPTER 1
In which Fain shows up with a lemon

Here's the whole story of how Fain the Gardener became Fain the Sorcerer. But I'll tell it quickly by leaving out the lies.

The King of Envashes offered a reward to whoever could awake his daughter, who had been sent to sleep by a necromancer. This was a tradition in those days: it gave everyone something to chat about other than pigs, and something to think about other than what was important.

Fain visited the court with the intention of squishing a half-lemon onto the nose of the princess, or perhaps simply shouting at her, or both. 'Or perhaps,' he thought, 'when the time comes, I won't be bothered to do either.' For Fain was a young man of his own mind and no-one else's.

But as Fain entered the audience room and saw the King awaiting on his throne, he happened to see also a miming, pranking moron who pulled faces at empty air and generally acted the fool. Enraged by the clown, Fain flew at him and smashed him to the floor, strangling the jangling jester as the whole court protested and claimed they were appalled. Finished, Fain stood to regain his composure as everyone cried out against him. 'He has destroyed the neck of the King's jester!' they announced, and called guards upon Fain. Fain was obliged to run outside, steal a beautiful horse and escape into the forest.

Though a mere labourer and odd-job man, Fain knew the business with the Princess was meant to distract the common people from rebelling against the King and other woes. 'With the spectacle I'm providing,' Fain thought, 'you would have thought the King would be grateful.'

Arriving at the mossy mouth of a cave, he was confronted by a ragged, one-armed man who staggered out with a jug jammed down over his head. 'You!' Fain shouted at the man, leaping from the horse and thwacking it into a run. 'Idiot! I must hide in your cave.'

'Take the jar from my head, and the cave is yours,' the man was saying as Fain knocked him aside and the jar smashed upon a rocky ledge. The tangle-bearded old man shouted 'Land of beer, nook of pine!' or something like that, but seemed quite happy. He picked up a few of the jar shards and scampered after Fain into the cave. Fain was explaining the anger he had incited at court by killing a mime.

'What was your crime?' croaked the old man.

'For the throttling of that stupid clown I'm being hunted by one and all—they'll probably follow the horse awhile, then double back and stab me.'

'Not you,' the old man chortled, and began dancing around the smashed pottery. 'For this urn is enchanted, and it falls to you, its destroyer in good faith, to receive its final three wishes. The old man you see cannot benefit from it—only others may. Choose!'

'Three wishes is it?' thought Fain. 'He's probably a total nutter but just in case, I'd better choose carefully.' For he knew such situations are notoriously sticky and fraught with unforeseen consequences. Magical literature was full of stories of impulsive dreamers asking for stupid things like 'an endless supply of sardines' and so on. Fain considered his options as carefully as he could with the threat of capture upon him. Then he piped up. 'Alright, old man—if this broken rubbish really does have the power to grant wishes, here are mine. One, that I can travel into the past to whatever time I wish, at will. Two, that I be given the knowledge of how to wake the Princess up at the castle. And three, that I have an endless supply of sardines.'

'You choose well, young stranger,' cackled the old lunatic.

Fain felt no different, and immediately wondered why he'd stood here in the cave mouth wasting his time with this dodgy relic.

But as he stormed out of the cave he saw the King's riders bearing down on him, the lead man drawing his sword with a yell. 'There's the villain now!'

As the sword drove toward him, Fain wished he could go back and do it all differently. The entire scene blurred as though he were falling backward over a cliff, the view rushing away from him. And indeed the wind was knocked out of him as he landed in the previous day, completely naked.

CHAPTER 2
In which Fain yells at the Princess

Fain knew at once what had happened—he had travelled back in time as he had wished, but his clothing hadn't. 'I've read about how tricky this wishing game can be. Genies seem to revel in deliberately misunderstanding the simplest orders.'

He looked for the old one-armed man at the cave-mouth but found nothing—not even the pieces of urn, because of course it had not yet been broken. He found a cottage nearby and stole a ragged shirt and trousers from the washing line. And he made his way to the castle, at which he had not yet disgraced himself. Nobody was interested in chasing him or ordering his death.

'You claim, like so many others, to be able to awake my daughter from her month-long slumber?' the King asked him without enthusiasm. The atmosphere at court was gloomy and despondent, courtiers glumly flicking the pennants. 'You realise she was enchanted by Hackler Thorn, the greatest sorcerer in the world?'

'I am the greater sorcerer, Your Majesty,' Fain lied. 'I can start waking her right away, if it's convenient.'

'You're a spirited young man. I hope, for your sake, that your confidence is well-founded.'

Fain was taken to the Princess's sick room, where she lay in a bed of yellow shot silk. Fain was surprised to find that she really was beautiful, not the bland blonde that princesses generally tend to be. She was all the colours of a playing card, with sky-white skin, jet black hair and a big mouth like a target. Fain thought on the matter of how to wake her, and found that he indeed possessed the knowledge, in accordance with his wish. 'Yes, I see what's happened—Thorn gave her a brief glimpse of a universe of possibilities. As a result she's utterly bored, your Majesty—by you, the court, the castle, the kingdom. Even at her young age it's years since she heard an original idea. I'll yell one in her ear and Bob's your royal uncle. Alright?' And crouching at the Princess's pale ear, he shouted 'Thursday and Saturday are the same day going under different names!'

And the Princess roused, much to the King's delight. 'What joy!' he cried. 'Send forth the word—the Princess is awake! We celebrate! Where is my jester?'

The jester pranced in to find his throat received and constricted by Fain, who shook him like a flag.

Pretty soon Fain was once again riding through the forest, the King's men in pursuit. 'At least,' he thought, 'I have released the Princess. But now that I've wrecked my chances at court by killing that mime again, I may as well carry out the other part of my plan—to meet with the old man and get another three wishes for myself. For as far as he's concerned, he hasn't met me yet.' He found the old man sitting in the cave mouth and thought to himself 'That moron will sit with that thing on his head for at least another day without my help.'

'You! Idiot!' he shouted at the man, leaping from the horse and thrashing it into a run. 'I must hide in your cave.'

'Take this jar from—'

Fain knocked him against the mossy wall, shattering the urn and freeing the man's head. The man cried 'When

15

you merely look, you pine!' or something like that. As the codger told him about the three wishes, Fain pretended it was the first he'd heard of all this. 'Only three wishes? Well, you can help me with a problem. I happen to possess the ability to travel into the past—now for my first wish I want to magic my garments back in time also, to save the inconvenience of appearing suddenly naked throughout history. Second, I of course need a constant supply of gold coins to appear in my pockets, no matter how much cash I remove. And third, I wish to travel instantly to the place where Thorn the Warlock enchanted the princess a month ago, yet an hour before it occurred.' For Fain could not stop thinking about the Princess.

'You choose well, young stranger,' cackled the old lunatic.

The day blinked and Fain stood completely naked in the massive audience hall of Thorn the Warlock.

CHAPTER 3

In which Fain pushes his luck with a real sorcerer

At first the Warlock seemed to be a pillar of innards, and then a rearing black serpent with transparent wings—and finally a fork-bearded skeleton, each bone of which was wrapped individually in its own snakeskin envelope. In the tradition of wizard kings, a living coat of arms was massed on the wall behind him, operative lengths of bone and muscle levering like a water clock. The Princess knelt near to Thorn's throne, her hands chained behind her.

'Who let the gardener in here?' bellowed the cloaked cadaver, and Fain thought the remark appropriate, as the hall's walls were encrusted with gargoyles so over-elaborate they looked like cabbages. 'Guards—take this wretch to the bird room and let him rot there.'

Fain was about to protest when he saw that the gargoyles were climbing down from the walls and crouching toward him.

Fain was still wondering about the clothing situation. 'Next time I'll have to specify that my clothes go with me from place to place, as well as from one time period to another. Does that magical madman keep landing me in it deliberately?'

Three of the gruesome sentinels took him down a maze of corridors past a hellhound kennel, a torture chamber, a green monster standing idle with an exploded face like a thistle, and a kitchen, and finally into the bird room, a high chamber with dove skeletons flying about the place and stone windows open to the air and sea. Fain was thrown into a domed cage and the door swung closed upon him. Two of the guards departed and the last, a hulking mutant with the scrolled horns of a goat, winched the cage upward to the ceiling. 'He can pull out your soul like a cork,' said the creature. 'You will die more slowly this way. My name is Tefnut. Goodbye.'

'Wait!' Fain called out. 'Give me a coat or shirt for warmth. That long-coat on the wall, perhaps.'

'Why?'

'I swear, Tefnut, the instant you give me ownership of that coat, I can reward you with a hundred gold coins.' For Fain knew he could draw endless cash from his pockets, if only he had any pockets.

'You're raving,' said Tefnut.

'Very well. Then tell me this—did this cage lay upon the floor a half-hour ago?'

'You should be in a cuckoo clock, I think,' laughed Tefnut.

Fain wished himself a half-hour back in time and fell from a point in mid-air, with no cage about him, for at this point in time the cage had yet to be winched upward. He was alone. Fain dressed himself in the coat and set out toward the great hall, stopping off at the kitchen to steal a cabbage. 'Invisibility would be useful for this lark,' he thought. 'I'll bear that in mind for the next time I meet the old cave-dweller.' As he arrived at the hall, Thorn was entering by the opposite door, dragging the Princess after him. Fain, with the outer layers of the cabbage shoved over his head, hunched over and shouted something like 'Master—the hellhounds have escaped, the apes are rebelling, a dragon has decided to bite your face, a tornado is coming, flowers everywhere have unclenched like fists, there's a fire in the kitchen and everywhere else, and the King has discovered the location of your lair and sent armies against you.'

'Well, I haven't *got* any apes,' said the warlock, 'but anyway I suppose I'll have to postpone my demand for marriage, m'dear.'

'I'm flattered,' said Fain, but the warlock was too busy to become enraged. He was giving the order to send out the fleet and guardgoyles were scampering in all directions. Fain grabbed the Princess and soon they were rushing aboard a warship and casting off. 'Gold coins for everyone in return for not killing me!' he cried, pulling cash from his pockets and ordering the crew to head toward Envashes. Soon they had left behind Thorn's island and his departing fleet.

At sunset, Fain met the Princess on deck. 'I seem fated to be hauled back and forth like cargo,' she snapped.

'My apologies, madam,' he told her. 'If I had planned ahead, this journey would not have been necessary. What is your name?'

'Aleksa.'

'How did Thorn bring you here?'

'He flew.'

'Flight, of course! And here I am wishing merely to keep my trousers on!'

'I beg your pardon?'

Fain felt he had squandered his wishes—and now he had to travel by normal means, at a normal rate, for a whole month before he would get another chance to add to his gifts.

And all the while the ship was heading in the wrong direction.

CHAPTER 4
In which Fain provokes the crew

In the middle of the Purge Sea it became clear that the crew hated Fain. He had dressed himself in a silk shirt and some baggy Turkish pantaloons, though he kept his coat on for warmth and for the production of the crew's wages. He had to haul hundreds of gold pieces from his pockets every morning to keep the monstrous sailors sweet, but the sheer accumulated weight of this bounty soon had the ship riding low in the water. 'Women are bad luck,' said the crew, looking at the Princess, 'as are men who dress like women,' they added, looking at Fain. They sneered that Fain's magic was weak compared to that of the mighty Thorn, and complained that they had nothing to eat but fish. Fain warned them to stand back and, announcing that he would give them abundant food by sorcery, conjured hundreds of sardines from thin air. Roaring with indignation, the crew threw him overboard.

Though Fain could swim, he realised that he was sinking like a stone, weighed down by the gold in his pockets. He jettisoned handful after handful of gold but the pockets continually re-filled as he descended through the dark brine. 'Though it's extremely useful in a thousand other situations,' he reminded himself pragmatically as he fell into unconsciousness.

CHAPTER 5
In which Fain meets a mermaid

Fain awoke in the upturned hulk of a galleon. He had been laid out on a table which floated near to a ceiling which had once been the floor. Boggle-eyed fish peered in through the cloudy windows and only seemed to find his shouting and arm-waving all the more fascinating. There was also a lot of sifting scum which didn't seem to have any firm idea where it wanted to go. Fain slumped back, feeling useless.

Becoming sleepy and glimpsing black underwater souls, Fain was awoken by a mermaid with scales of green silver, a mother-of-pearl face and golden-ochre eyes. For a day the mermaid sustained the air in the wreck by hauling down the inverted shell of a giant mollusc and upending it inside the cabin. The following morning she took Fain to the beach of a small island.

For weeks Fain lived here. Sleeping on the beach was like being in the palm of nature's hand. The mermaid showed him seaweed which, when the observer made the small effort to forget that it was seaweed, showed itself to be a ribbon of runes. She taught him to breathe underwater by explaining that it was the same as not breathing when out of water— something millions of mortal men had achieved. They swam over the ember glow of coral reefs. Here trailed the fine biology of lace creatures, varicose jellyfish and honeycomb skeins of yellow which the mermaid seemed to tell him in her slow, low, bubbling voice were part of the sea's mind. She taught him to see the liquid gold architecture of ocean currents as leaves of art flitted past. Fishes with silver throats poured through the old slimy ship offshore, a galleon forgotten into murk. It looked different to him now, the furred cabin a good dark shell for shy eels and a landscape for snails like walking doorknobs. It seemed books, too, were improved by the sea—dipped into it, even the slimmest plumped up.

But like a fool—indeed so like a fool he was one—Fain found a way to escape this sun trap. Laying in the shallow surf with the mermaid one day, the sea leaving hieroglyphs in the sand around them, he heard her tell of a conch shell through which he could speak into the dreams of any person anywhere. 'None of my scant magic can transport me across the world,' he thought. 'But I can call someone who does have that power.'

As the mermaid looked on with a puzzled smile, he spoke into the shell: 'Hackler Thorn is so insignificant no-one even bothers to really hate him, and what serves as his brain is a sort of thin gas such as you'd find ghosting in the ribcage of a chicken dead for nine years. So says Fain the Sorcerer!'

Fain retrieved his coat and clothing, kissed the mermaid's hard glossy head and told her to hide in the sea. He felt something strange in his belly as he watched her broad silver tail slap out of view beneath the green waves. And he was still wondering about it when Hackler Thorn landed on the beach astride a black rose dragon. Today Thorn was spectral and glabrous like a newborn moon-baby. He also had fangs where a milder man would have had eyelashes, and these clicked when he blinked—which was three times during the following exchange.

'Fain. I am not alone in wondering whether you are a spud. Yours is the stupidity of which men have known by fabulous report alone—until now.'

'Thank you.'

'It seems idiots no longer mask their identities but boast of their ignorance. I've a longstanding policy of clouting such creatures to the grave.'

'I'll not fight with you, nor your male equivalent.'

Thorn blinked for the third time, and then produced a grey metal sphere from his saddlebag. 'Do you know what this is?'

'Some sort of parsnip?'

'This is a jailhead, used for carrying souls away like kittens in a sack.' Thorn touched a bung or valve near its underside. 'Welcome.'

Fain found himself standing in a small room with a hundred other people, up to his neck in murky soup.

CHAPTER 6

In which Fain swims through human soup

It was a low-domed chamber filled with murky fluid and a hand-picked assortment of gibbering wretches. In the soup up to their necks, they wore hats in a variety of styles. 'Welcome, newly hopeless,' said the nearest grey man, who seemed relatively cheerful. 'And here are your knitting and sewing materials.'

'What for?'

'For making hats, of course. One must keep up appearances.'

Fain took the sewing kit. 'Thank you, kind sir—I hope to outshine every bonnet here. But is not escape the more urgent matter? There must be an entrance to this cell.'

'Perhaps, but it is not above the soup. And who would want to submerge and see the terrible state our bodies must be in? I have seen occasional matters floating on the surface which I have made an effort not to recognise.'

'The place has stained his wits,' thought Fain, and asked aloud, 'Don't you find this stinking place unpleasant?'

'Yes, it's quite limited. Hackler Thorn is one who has, on balance, lived a fortunate life, and so believes that a so-called "living hell" is a punishment different from the life of an average man. We howl here, occasionally, so as not to make him wonder. But otherwise it is an acceptable domicile. I served Hackler Thorn.'

'You were in his army?'

'Not me,' said the grey man. 'I spent a short time pouring candles—a very short time, as I was a bartender and my little trick and its solid aftermath were not appreciated. I made the mistake of handing one such undrinkable clot to a thirsty stranger who turned out to be Thorn. Why was a candlemaker working in an alehouse? I had fallen hard because of an artistic enterprise, an innovation whereby I painted portraits in wax so that over time they would become jowled and wrinkled like their subjects. Oh I'm baffled now by my actions—who wants to see such stuff? And so, here I am.'

'The sooner I accept local custom,' thought Fain, 'the longer I shall remain. Not every contract is sealed by waking consent.'

Diving beneath the broth, he swam between the prisoners, many mere stands of bone loosely adrift with pale and soggy meat. Breathing easy as a merman in the murk, Fain saw the inner side of the entry valve, the size of a barrel lid. Grabbing the rim, he pulled himself headfirst toward it.

Fain felt himself expanding like a blowfish and, once he had his bearings, found that he was dropping through the air thousands of feet above the ground.

CHAPTER 7
In which Fain falls from a height of thirty thousand feet

Fain's belly tipped over as he dropped away from Hackler Thorn's dragon, which flew on unawares. Wet mist pelted upward and he saw a teal green land tilting several leagues below him.

'Ah well,' he thought. 'We rot to something the size of a penny, then to less. I shall make the process my main priority after I hit the ground. I'll out-rot the best!'

But then, recalling a fayre stall magician he had seen leaping from a platform with a black star-spangled sheet above him to catch air and slow his fall, he twisted off his coat and tried holding it above him. The arms would need closing up. Fain had just taken out the needle and thread given him by the prisoner when the battering air tore the entire arrangement out of his hands and it flapped into the sky above him.

As the drop accelerated he thought, 'Next time I meet the old man I must ask for the ability to fly.' But there would be no next time! And realising the gifts he already had, Fain thought himself an hour into the past. He was still in mid-air, but his stomach rolled as if he had only just begun to fall. The velocity had not transferred into the past—he had simply appeared in mid-air at a standing start, and begun to drop again toward his bloody death. He went back another hour, and the same thing happened. 'Hardly an improvement,' he thought. 'I suppose I could live this way for a while, falling haltingly through the sky and eating an occasional sardine. But eventually exhaustion would claim my attention and I would fail to save myself.'

Then realising that at this rate he would enter the darkness of the previous night, he went back only a minute, feeling the same stop and gradual acceleration downward. Repeating this process, he became better acquainted with the lay of the land below him, an antlike horse and cart on a road, woodland like smoke, and a castle which stood off to the west. He was reminded of Envashes and the Princess. 'At least those sailors won't harm her,' he thought. 'As they know Thorn values her. Because I rescued her before she was enchanted, I don't get my reward—but I don't care as long as she's impressed.' After a bit of this, he felt more at home in the air and his body was no longer panicking of its own accord at having nothing to depend on.

Hearing what seemed to be the scream of a woman, he looked up to see the small figure of himself, approaching rapidly. He went back another hour and decided to simply brace himself for a full fall. Perhaps a second before sitting at great speed upon that track next to the forest, he might wish himself five minutes into the past and plump down quite comfortably.

He glimpsed the blur of the road but seemed to be coasting toward the trees, travelling faster, surely, than any surviving man ever had. Touching the treetop, he wished himself an hour back. He began to fall as though he had merely toppled from an upper branch, thereby sustaining only one-hundred-and-eleven breaks to the bones of his body.

CHAPTER 8
In which Fain meets a faceless stranger

Fain lay amid leaves and broken branches on the forest floor, screaming as much as his shattered ribs would allow. A cloaked figure was knelt by him, tipping a small colourless bottle to Fain's lips. 'Absentia draft,' the hooded stranger whispered. 'A posit tincture, based upon the notion of there being either no creator, or one which is competent and efficient. Either way, the result is much less pain, and extremely rapid healing.'

Soon Fain was riding beside the cloaked man on the wooden seat of a horse-drawn cart. He felt better than he ever had, and for some reason felt no curiosity about the hooded figure. 'We approach the city of Camovine,' said the man. 'Beware the local autarch. He keeps a mirror by which you may travel far, and he would use it to evacuate the town if he could, but a gewgaw lives within, which eats down those who enter and spits them out like apple cores.'

'I'm hungry,' said Fain.

'If I'm hungry I pull up one of the earth's veins, slit it open and drink from it. What else do *you* do?'

'Kill a warthog.'

'Which of itself has drunk from the veins of the earth.'

'I should have said "try" to kill a warthog. They're hard to find, and even harder to catch. To kill, perhaps impossible. It's the same with bears.'

'I know it is.'

'So this earth vein business might not be such a crazy idea.'

'Not crazy at all. Just boring. Lacking adventure, and thus creating no stories. And because it creates no stories, it is a wisdom repeatedly lost and only by chance rediscovered. True wisdom is like that. Not spectacular. This is Camovine. I leave you here.'

'Thanks for the ride,' Fain called after the covered cart as it passed into the city. Some sort of celebration seemed to be underway. A hectically happy gatekeeper told Fain he had the good fortune to arrive in the city on the day of Saint ExStrainia's Festival.

CHAPTER 9
In which Fain offends the Autarch

'The Festival of Saint ExStrainia,' the Gatekeeper explained, stepping back apparently so that he could shout all the louder. 'One day he raised his eyebrows in surprise and they kept on going, flying over his domed head and away like two caterpillars caught in a strong wind.'

'Hardly seems to justify this level of celebration,' thought Fain as he entered the frenzied city. Everywhere he looked revellers in green and purple costumes spoke sarcasm from far lands and were sent into fits of sneezing by rare spices. Optimists harassed him with reclamation and others offered to tattoo his eyes so that he would see beauty wherever he looked. But they all danced away before he could respond.

The scent of strong ginger and blue moon tobacco assailed his senses. Dyed ashes stained the air. The streets seemed to have been widened recently, the chalk walls of houses carved into or entire houses destroyed to create open squares. A surfeit of fortune? A procession of old failed instincts merely? But Fain knew that in the heart there is no such thing as exaggeration. A town crier was wagging a bell and crying:

'Oh yay. Oh yay. The Autarch is well pleased and expects you to feel the same way.'

A fellow whose costume was tagged with red and

yellow knots laughed uproariously at this and Fain approached him. 'You sir!' he shouted.

Now that Fain was closer to the man, he could see that he was sobbing desperately. How had Fain thought he was laughing? But having drawn back a little, the man again seemed to be shrieking in celebration like those around him. It was like a trick picture Fain had once seen of a white vase against a black background, which on a second look changed to two faces opposing each other.

Fain was standing next to a chiming roundabout of citizens riding candy-coloured horses—the laughing, shouting riders grew gaunt with despair as they hove near, then swept by into public enjoyment again. Fain was feeling more vertigo than he had when he fell from the sky.

The man in the knot costume bolted down the street and Fain pursued him, finally grabbing the fellow and barging him against a wall. Up close, he could see that the man was in tears of utter despair. 'In our belltower,' he sobbed, 'is the bell of a jellyfish. We don't know how to organise anything.'

'What's going on here?'

'We're exhausted,' grated the man, then thrust himself from Fain's grasp, capering lightly away with a carefree smile.

Everything was smothered in faded and sickly bunting. On the way to the castle Fain tore some away from a bandstand and the wood beneath was cindered, flaking charcoal.

The castle's audience room was all gloom and a vastness of pillars. The Autarch was sat on a vulturine oak throne against a wall hung with dark green velvet. He was a fat man wearing a stellate, mechanical- looking crown and was flanked by several smirking idiots.

'Hail, Your Majesty—I have come to witness your famous antics.'

'You pay me no obeisance?'

'To do so would seem a pointless courtesy. You seem obese enough already.'

'I unfortunately ate my salad days immediately, because I thought that's what they were for.'

'Of course! How could it be otherwise. I hear tell that you own a very deep mirror. I would like to swim into it as far as I can.'

'Sir, your remarks have amazed us all. And we will devote as many minutes as are required for you to produce the proof.'

One of the Autarch's cronies piped up. 'Rather than speculate, let's attack the fellow and see what happens.'

'Perhaps we could attack him in an *encouraging* way?' another suggested.

'Let him see we understand why he's startled,' said a third.

'That's a plan,' the Autarch nodded, and turned to Fain. 'You are to be executed, young man—what do you say to that?'

'It'll hurt, which will surprise no-one.'

'Surprise? You young scallywag. But truly, in cases like this we can make use of a new distraction.'

'There seems enough distraction outside, Your Majesty, on this Festival day.'

'We have the Festival every day. Ours is a fair and fortunate city.'

'Oh yes? I hear you've got a squid in your belltower.'

'You interpret this as a cry for help? Perhaps you are correct. A silent cry, as it must be. The fact is, we are harassed by a particularly pernicious and inconvenient dragon of the fire-breathing, sacrifice-requiring sort. Bring us the dead body of the dragon, and you may explore the mirror you mentioned.'

'Your confidence in me is baseless but I'll do my best. How old would you say the dragon is?'

'Two thousand years.'

'And how long do the buggers usually live?'

'Three thousand. He's not likely to just conk out, if that's what you're hoping.'

'What do they eat?'

'People.'

'Other than people. A ham sandwich?'

'Rummed honey. But it won't come to that. He'll bolt you down that gilded neck like the crack of a whip.' The Autarch couldn't stop laughing, but Fain doubted it was real mirth. When the Autarch stepped down and approached Fain, a worry crease like an archery slit appeared on the Autarch's face; closer still, and a despairing wretch stood there, as much life in his eye as in that of a rocking horse. 'Here is a map of our kingdom, a mere copy, as it shall surely be burnt. It shows the location of the beast's cave.' The Autarch lumbered back again, and these last words were barely coherent amid the liquid splutter of his hilarity.

CHAPTER 10
In which Fain fights a dragon

Spotlessly clean bones were scattered around the cave mouth and from that mouth flowed a grey smoke which was twisting among itself like a crowd of grey squirrels. Fain entered the cave, pushing the barrow before him.

The cave smelt of sulphur and titanic friction. Fain trundled through snapping wrists and ribs, having to slow and speed up as the light in the cave flared and dimmed in a regular rhythm. Reaching a broad ledge which formed a gallery around the walls of the master pit, he peered down.

The dragon didn't look finished. This yellow worm with thirteen wings had tiny human eyes like a whale and many white stalk legs facing the wrong way. It was balled up like a centipede, coal-light heating and cooling between a million wolf teeth as it breathed in sleep.

Fain tipped the barrow forward, rummed honey pouring like lava upon the beast's tail. Then he descended to the floor of the pit, took ahold of the honeyed tail tip and hauled it to the dragon's jaws, pressing it to the cage of teeth. In sleep the monster finally opened the tall maw, and Fain fed the tail in. The dragon began to eat its own tail, as Fain fed more inside. Fain was terrified that at any moment the creature would awake and inflict harsh retribution.

And when the first of its thirteen wings reached the

back of its throat, the dragon's tiny eyes flipped open—the beast reared up and the twelve remaining wings batted suddenly out like holly leaves. It released the roar of a thousand churchbells.

Fain scampered up the gallery aside the pit and ducked behind the barrow, raising it like a shield so quickly that it flipped away into the pit. He rose again like a saint as the dragon sucked sparking fire into the furnace of its mouth in preparation to blast him. But instead of fire the dragon vomited a great deal of what it had just eaten—which was in part rummed honey but mostly the yet undigested matter of its own tail.

'And so here I stand,' thought Fain, 'his favourite food covered in his fondest dressing. Body, farewell.'

Then he felt a turmoil of heat broiling around him.

CHAPTER 11
In which Fain enters a mirror

Fain walked empty-handed back into town. He had nothing to show for his quest but a smoking crust of fire-proof matter from the dragon's own body. Should he add permanent fire-proofing to his gifts? As he entered the Autarch's court again, he pondered the tally of his requirements.

The Autarch scrutinised the steaming human ember before him. 'No skull or other artefact to prove you have slain the dragon? Ah well, many are the friendships forged during an execution.'

Fain concluded his ruminations. 'My word,' he solemnly and quietly decided. 'Is my bond.'

'Don't understand me so quickly, Your Majesty,' he announced aloud. 'While you've been sitting around eating roast larks, I've set the dragon alight and slung its remains on a cart which you will find outside. Except a bit of its tail.'

Everyone convened outside the castle and found a cart upon which the scorched, reduced body of the dragon lay coiled and gruesome.

Everyone seemed to drop their disguise at once. They were a people who had cried so much that deep vertical channels below the eyes had become an inherited characteristic.

'Brilliant,' said the Autarch. 'A stunning kick in the

pants for me, of course. I suppose it may become a costly nightmare but you've earned your reward. Quick, laddie—before I change my mind.'

The Autarch led Fain into a black and silver chamber at the rear of the castle. It was arrayed with standing mirrors.

'I collect them,' he said, indicating various acquisitions. 'This is a torrent mirror—I use it to store past information that may or may not be useful later. It's like an infinite cupboard. This is a widow glass, a mirror of tears. Tears of sadness, or joy I suppose, depending on your view of widowhood.' It was a mirror of flowing mercury in which Fain's image undulated, looking startled. 'And here's my marrow glass, which in good condition could replace one's body while leaving all illness within the glass.' A rough, scapular sort of bone had grown half out of the mirror. 'This is the sort of nonsense I have to contend with. It's too old.'

He halted Fain beside two tall mirrors which stood facing each other. Both had a blackstone frame of a thousand curlicues as if worms had been casting in liquid jet.

Fain leaned cautiously in to view one of the mirrors. A recessive tunnel of frames curved away from him. His own reflection was absent. But he saw, halfway down the tunnel, a thin grey arm like a stick, poking out between one reflected frame and another like an insect caught on a window. It quickly withdrew.

Fain turned to the Autarch. 'I'm aware nobody has survived this conveyance,' he said. 'But what if it spits me out alive?'

'You will be banished from my kingdom.'

'This is your guarantee?'

The Autarch did not reply.

'Rigid disapproval eh? I had best begin my experiment.'

Fain stepped between the mirrors. Casting no reflection in the bending tunnel of frames, he stepped forward into the mirror before him and walked down the tunnel, stepping over the frame of each reflected mirror as he went. A glance behind him afforded no clue as to his progress. Turning forward again he was confronted with a chiselled little beast. At first it seemed the creature wore a white helmet designed to simulate the segmentations of a fruit, then Fain saw that its head was all teeth, a white density of interleaving fangs which made up a strange ivory sphere. The arrangement seemed to be constantly revolving and rearranging like the grinding faces of a mill. Its body was a sheaf of grey insectile gears.

'As empires fatten on pretence,' it said, 'must you dine upon the scraps of its glamour?'

Fain felt a whole shadow float up inside him and disperse.

'You surprise me,' said the gremlin. 'You may pass.'

'Then you don't mean to gnaw me down to a chog?'

'No,' said the gremlin. 'You are honest and, additionally, fresh-minted from some sort of pledge.'

'What manner of creature are you, if you don't mind my asking?'

'I am *now* a mote elf called Glut. I *was* an ironical writer called Glut, ever given to tricks of reflection and a constant avoidance of taking up one position on any matter. For my sins a sorcerer named Drake the Adept made me this mirror's gatekeeper, where I must see and give credit to the truth of things, and know that such truths exist. Only the honest are granted safe passage. After allowing passage three times, I will be freed. Did

Drake know how rare that quality is? Was he that cruel? I have been imprisoned sixty years, and you are the first I will allow to continue the journey.'

Fain suggested that Camovine might be a more likely prospect now that its citizens had less to evade, but the gremlin was scornful. 'You'd expect them to accept certain realities. But I've found even the most meagre-resourced fellows employ their last gasp to evade those. I remember one who lay on his back with his head raised and used such a gasp to puff his belly up, so for his last few seconds he couldn't see the horizon. He'd been planning it for years but when the moment came he had to arrange it in a hurry.'

The mote elf produced a small box of polished tin, lifting the lid to display a space of fizzing red before snapping it shut again. 'These are veracity spiders, terrible allies of my old trade. They test the truth of a thing by swarming upon it until it is devoured, but taking up the true shape of the thing for a short while. Take them.' He handed the box to Fain, then pointed with a crop-like arm down the curving tunnel behind him. 'You will arrive where you wish to go.'

Fain thanked the imp and began walking down the tunnel. Looking aside, he saw far silverine leagues beyond each frame. Then he tripped, falling into the mud outside the King of Envashes' palace.

CHAPTER 12
In which Fain offends the King of Envashes

'My first audience with the King was about a month after the princess was taken for enchantment,' thought Fain. 'I think I am a little later than that now.' He called to a passing farmer. 'Tell me—is the Princess here? And if so is she enchanted in any way?'

'Pah! The Princess was stolen away weeks ago by a sorcerer.'

'Thorn?'

'Fain. And she's not been seen since.'

'Did you say "Fain" took her away?'

'That's what the King's expensive new soothsayer has discovered.'

'Really. And what does this soothsayer call himself?'

'Charlie. They gave him a liver and asked that he read the future in it. He declared with absolute certainty that the liver's former owner would soon die if he or she was not dead already. It gave everyone the shivers. Better proof of magic there never was.'

Fain entered the King's court covered in mud and dragon vomit.

'What is this creature?' the King demanded. 'How did he get in here?'

'Once again, Your Majesty, I have confounded your great raspberry of a head. And where's this soothsayer I've heard about? Surely not this fellow with the constellation cape and sharpened chin?'

The soothsayer whirled upon Fain and declared: 'This is Fain the Sorcerer—he who stole away the Princess!'

'On the contrary!' shouted Fain with all the ridiculous drama he could summon. 'You took the Princess, and are Hackler Thorn in disguise!'

Fain took out the tin box of crimson veracity spiders, opened the lid and threw it at the soothsayer, who seemed paralysed by their swarming attentions. Amid the shrieks of the court he was bitten down until all that remained was a sort of grandfather clock with lungs, four rod-like legs pitching it to the ground and two arms of real human bone. It had a fist-sized dice for a heart and a spinal column of coins. Its face was an ivory fan painted with the false eyes common to butterfly wings. All had noticed that the thing was insincere, a mere reaction, but at court this was the very genius of its camouflage.

The strange construction began to crumble and dissolve as the spiders died, but before it faded Fain glimpsed a sort of meaty tube like an umbilical cord which fed from it, looped over a candelabrum and descended to the head of the King's jester. The jester started up when Fain saw him, and a black spike pronged out of its forehead in readiness for combat. 'Thorn!' Fain gasped, and in moments was throttling the warlock.

'He has killed our madcap!' yelled the King.

'Not for the first time,' Fain bragged, admiring his handiwork before recalling the need to run.

'All well and good for today,' he thought as he dashed down the entrance galley, 'but in seeking more gifts I must needs travel back to a time when that annoying fool is alive again.' And it seemed clear that, just as a punishment in the present undoes no crimes in the past, no matter what changes Fain affected in the past, Thorn would proceed to more or less the same point in the present. Fain could not, after all, change the man's nature. But he wished he understood the root of it.

He wished himself into the past, surprising a few guards as he appeared out of thin air a week earlier, sprinting from the palace.

CHAPTER 13
In which Fain begins a bar brawl

Feeling a sudden thirst for ale, Fain walked through the forest and found the old man roasting chestnuts outside the cave.

'You! Idiot!' he shouted at the man. 'Have you any ale?'

'Take this jar from my head and I will—'

Fain knocked him against the mossy wall, shattering the urn and freeing the man's head. The man called out some nonsense which sounded like 'Fan your fear to put with mine!' or something like that, and then told him about the three wishes. Again Fain pretended it was the first he'd heard of all this. 'So—three wishes! Well, having thought about it for a second: I wish to be able to become invisible whenever I wish—including the clothes I am wearing at the time I make the wish, old man! Secondly, I wish to have the ability to transport myself from one place to another—with clothing intact! And, thirdly, I want to be able to travel forward in time—while retaining my clothes!'

'You choose well, young stranger,' cackled the old lunatic.

Fain immediately wished himself transported to an alehouse he had heard tell of in town. Nothing happened but that he for some reason started walking away from the cave. He stopped, angry, and walked back to the cave mouth. 'Betrayal old man? What of the power to transport myself from place to place?'

'Simply place one leg in front of the other alternately, young one. Though I confess, I felt sure you possessed this power already.'

'And let me guess—you also believed I already had the ability to travel forward in time?'

'Are you not constantly doing so?'

'Two gifts wasted!' Fain thought. Should he slip back in time and get more immediately? How long did the old man have that thing on his head? Days? Weeks? How stupid could a man be? What sort of cheated existence had marooned the old man in a cave from which he dealt such perversity?

Feeling he could not abide the man any more, Fain strode off to the river, where he washed the dragon grime from his body. Then he went back into Envashes town to visit a barber, where his head was restored to a more human appearance. And finally he went to an inn, where he ordered several meals, paying with the inexhaustible gold from his pockets. He delicately relished the beer as though it were a crime. Satisfied, he leaned back in his chair. A great feeling of lethargy filled him. Must he travel over a thousand years into the future to deal with the dragon? 'Perhaps,' he thought momentarily, 'my word need not be my bond.' But upon glancing at a mirror, he saw an empty wedge develop across his neck and a skull grinning from his face. 'My word is my bond!' he shrieked aloud, and all was well with his reflection and his intent.

Fain looked around him. Above the fireplace was a painting of blind black sharks in a bright yellow sea. Strolling over, Fain scrutinised the dark signature in its corner—Drake the Adept. An old crone, her face like a whiskery potato, stabbed his shoulder with her chin and said 'Something eldritch aint it? There's another over there—by the door.'

Fain went with her to the other, smaller painting—this portrayed a triangular, pointed building with a saucer-like eye near its base. The structure seemed to be in the centre of a lush, curlicued forest grown from red earth. 'What do you know about this Drake?'

'It's said these are not imagined scenes but a record of places he visited on his travels. He's now a powerful wizard. Have you really never heard of him?'

'No,' said Fain, and began to feel numb. He was choking, his throat a fizzing absence. Black blood filled his mouth. 'I mean yes,' he said, and swallowed. 'A strange gremlin creature once mentioned him to me.'

'Sit down, young man, you look ill. And let me read your palm—I will see all of your past and future in it!'

Before Fain knew what was happening, the old hag had his palm unrolled and was tracing lines in it. Her finger began tracing circles and she started to shudder and shriek. 'Spirals! Spirals!' She bolted up and whirled around the room, batting at invisible designs and knocking over the furniture. She pointed at him. 'He's Fain, a spiral beyond his life!'

What with a crone babbling words weird as green carrots and pointing his way, Fain attracted the attention of a ready mob, at the head of which a hod carrier stated their case: 'I know of a jackass called Fain who pulls spuds in a village miles from here. And I've heard tell of a wizard called Fain who wears fine clobber and spends gold like a penny. Which might you be?'

'Fain the Sorcerer,' said Fain, without thinking or standing.

'That's the Fain who abducted the princess,

45

according to the King's soothsayer Charlie.'

'Already?' Fain blurted.

'Hold him!' shouted the hod man, at which Fain became as thin as soup and then vanished altogether, his chair tipping back to hit the floor.

But Fain, standing to dash invisibly from the inn, found that he was plunged into darkness. He realised he was blind, and with a screech of fear, re-materialised again, rubbing his eyes. The mob, surprised but with motives supported by what they had seen, rushed at him. Fain ducked aside, disappearing. 'Where are you?' roared the hod man.

'Over here,' Fain called from the door, unable to lie. He reappeared, mortified. Throwing gold with one hand and sardines with the other, he faded away again. Someone entering the door was pushed aside by thin air and, believing that he was under attack, threw himself at the hod man.

CHAPTER 14
In which Fain visits the Pyramid of Puva

'It seems,' Fain thought, walking away from the inn a day earlier, 'my powers make it more difficult than ever to be among my fellow men.'

Why had he been blind when invisible? Fain realised it must be to do with the light which brings pictures into the eye to be captured there. If the eyes are invisible the light will pass straight through without stopping. 'Perhaps I need some guidance from a wizard mentor such as this Drake I keep hearing about.'

Fain bought a horse, a travelling sack, rope, a lantern and other supplies, and left Envashes town. Reaching the cave in the forest, Fain found the old man sitting nearby, with the vase still in place. 'You! Old idiot! Need any help with the vase?' He dismounted and smashed the vase with a single kick.

The greybeard shouted 'Damn you, I will cook you fine!' or something like that, grinning. 'This urn is enchanted, and it falls to you to receive its final three wishes!'

'Tell me, old man, are you Drake the Adept?'

'No. You have two wishes left.'

Fain was about to curse, but had to hold his tongue because the wishing was in play. 'I want to be able to become invisible at will, including my clothing, while still being able to see. I want to visit the place in the

picture in the Duke's Tongue Inn in Envashes town—
not the picture of the black whales, not the one of the
jouster with fruit on his lance, not the one of the pig, I
mean the picture of the triangular building in the forest,
and I don't want to be inside the painting itself, but
at the location which inspired the picture, and fully
clothed please.'

'You choose well, young stranger,' cackled the old
lunatic.

And though Fain had intended to go back in time
immediately to harvest more wishes from the old man,
he found himself instead standing before the massive
pyramid in the heat and birdcalls of a foreign jungle.

'I am so stupid,' Fain thought, shaking his head,
and before doing anything else, sat down to decide what
his next wishes would be. 'Future travel, instant land
travel, and knowing the location of Hackler Thorn at
any time, wherever he is.' Making a mental note of this,
he stood again and walked toward the pyramid.

Fain climbed the broad stone steps toward the dish-
eye. Reaching it, he saw the legend around the iris which
read: AS A CHEAT WITH LITTLE TIME DISSEMBLES
UNTO UNION. Fain waited until nightfall, using the time
to find a sturdy log and drag it up the steps. By nightfall
the iris seemed to have swollen a little, and a small hole
had appeared at its centre. Fain stood before the eye
and began to flatter it, stating that it was beautiful,
perfect in its roundness, and that he understood it.
He wished he could add that he and it were the same,
that they would be together always, but his recent oath
prevented him. Yet the iris had grown larger and the
hole at its centre had revolved open. Fain braced the
entrance with the log and ducked through.

Inside, the stone of the passage wall was cool and

moist, granular beneath his hand. Raising his lamp, he saw that the wall was patterned with jigsaw curlicues which he realised were the outlines of a thousand stone geckos, ingeniously interlocked. He emerged into a titanic vaulted hall, the pointed ceiling lost in mist. The building was completely hollow, and lit inadequately here and there with flaming torches. Fain noticed that even these sheer inner walls were complicated with interlocking lizards.

Against the far distant opposite wall there was something like steps and a throne. Dowsing his lamp, he decided to become invisible. He was glad to find that he could still see what was around him, but found that not being able to see his own feet made it difficult to walk. Several minutes later he reaches the steps, which led up to a square head on a stained stone pedestal. It almost resembled a huge stone owl. Fain found it was near to impossible to climb the stairs without visible legs, and re-appeared in sheer frustration halfway up the steps.

'Tomb robbers have cored the marrow of this place,' boomed the square granite head. Fain noticed that it had a single round eye. 'What do you hope to gain here?'

'Information about the sorcerer Drake.'

'I am Suvramizana, idol of time. Drake the Adept was drawn here by the Sertris Eye. He expected, wrongly, that it related to his craft, because the eyeball happens to be the only way one disguised sorcerer can recognise another.'

'I don't understand,' said Fain, who had arrived on the platform on which the pedestal stood. He had to crane his head to see the sad, flickering stone face. There was a stone teardrop suspended from the oyster eye.

'Your eyeballs turn upside down when you become a true sorcerer. Being completely round, it is the one part of the body which can be inverted without an external observer being any the wiser.'

Fain doubted this, as he had met people whose entire face could be turned upside-down without looking much different, but he kept silent on the matter. 'How long have you been here?'

'Since the excommunication of the sky,' chimed the statue mournfully. 'Time is not what people believe it is. It is the colour which is always present but which cannot be seen until truthfully named. Its name is not "time". Decisions of life can be forged in a moment—the contours and notches of the moment will tell you a great deal about the man.' The echoing voice faded, a pause. 'Yet I cannot sense any such thing with you. I can taste the dissolution and miscommunications surrounding a person who has begun life in the middle.'

'As opposed to what?'

'There are, now and again, folk born with the knowledge of what the world's judgement of them will be after they die; they know what their life's legacy will be. These people are remarkably content, whatever their circumstances.'

'Even if their legacy is one of failure, or a life of pain and torture? Why are they contented?'

'Because, unlike everyone else, they know precisely where they fit within the story.'

'Why would anyone want to fit within a story? I'm glad I don't know, and if I knew, I'd smash my way out of it.'

'You seem nervous when I speak of time.'

'Not at all.'

'I know what time smells like. And you've been

through it—the wrong way.' There was a moment's silence, a trickle of water as the statue digested its own thoughts. 'I see now. You're a bit of Fain the Sorcerer. From not even a tenth of the way along—no wonder I didn't recognise you. Fain is like a garter snake with a different flavour in each stripe.'

'Where is Drake the Adept now?'

'Take a look at my head. It's a perfectly square block, with a different face on four surfaces. Each face has a different outlook and expression. Every five hundred years it rotates so that the next face looks forward and becomes active.'

'What happens when you've rotated four times and gone back to the first one again?'

'By that time I've forgotten what it was, or convinced myself it was something else. But that's not important. What does the next face look like? The one to my left. Quick now! In a mirror I can only see the front one. And my worshippers are forbidden to gaze upon the face of the future. Look to my left face! Will I be happy? Tell me and I will reveal the location of Drake the Adept.'

Fain edged around and looked at the face on that side of the cube. It too had a single eye, and was grimacing as if Suvramizana had just tasted a piece of bark.

Fain thought about it, and cleared his throat. 'I assure you, asked such a question in such circumstances, most men would certainly declare it the happiest face in the world.'

'Excellent,' said the statue. 'Drake dwells in the Valley of Smohalla in the land of Zerzan. He lives behind the rain. To find him go East, cross the Bridge of Exasperation, the Black Desert, and on. Go now.'

Fain descended the steps, crossed the massive pointed chamber and lit his lantern for the walk through the outer passage, but found as he walked through it that daylight was shining from outside. Time had passed differently inside the pyramid.

As Fain neared the glaring exit he heard a small voice to his left. 'I want out,' it said.

'Who are you?' Fain asked.

'A gecko called Hex. Here I am. Step back a little. Look at me—I'm twenty-seventh from the floor. This is terrible. Can I come with you?'

'Why?' Fain whispered uncertainly, and glanced back at Suvramizana's chamber.

'Would you want to be locked into a pattern like this? They won't miss me. If the structure's worth a damn it'll do without little me won't it?'

'Very well, lizard. But hurry.'

With a little puff of masonry dust one of the grey lizards popped out of the wall, clinked to the dirt floor and skittered up Fain's body to perch on his shoulder, where it immediately flushed through with the exact colour of Fain's coat.

As he turned to leave, Fain noticed that other lizards had begun popping from the wall around Hex's vacated space, until that entire wall began falling away like a million-piece jigsaw tipped sideways.

'They've all gotten the same idea!' piped Hex into Fain's ear as Fain ran from the pyramid, dashing down the hill of steps as the pyramid began to crumple behind him, clouds of buff dust blasting from rectangular gashes. A landslide of grey lizards poured down the steps, but when Fain looked behind him he saw that they were already interlocking again, clotting in a zigzag of multi-levelled terraces as the pyramid settled.

CHAPTER 15

In which Fain crosses the Bridge of Exasperation

Fain walked among trees which bore fruit like resinous organic gems, until he reached a chasm of steam. A thin bridge of wood and rope receded into mist. The Bridgekeeper had an espaliered head, a bone lattice through which veins and tendons were woven like vines. 'Step out upon this bridge,' it said, 'and you will meet a challenger who will ask five questions. Answer correctly, and you may pass.' As Fain stepped onto the bridge he saw that several threads of gutting fed into it from the Bridgekeeper, veins twisting into the hand rope.

Fain peered ahead as he walked, expecting the challenge at any moment. An hour later he was still walking without obstruction through hot wet steam. Soon the smoke was dry and far beneath the bridge a landscape of red-black lava crawled like luminous molasses.

Sunset rivers were skirting debris which seemed to topple without ever reaching the ground. Crusts cracked open to weep gold, heaving piles of palaces with folk still at the windows. A watchtower of crumbling salt dissolved into the tangle of angled troughs which were once streets. Mangled treasure and molten shortcuts were folding over each other, the terrain eating itself. Watching, Fain could not tell whether this was truly disarray. He had a spectacular headache. Before him was always a flashing sheet of shredded air, and the receding bridge. The same was behind him. He continued walking forward through a drizzle of white ash. 'Remember to ask for the gift of flying,' he reminded himself, ticking off gifts as he watched creation forever unknitting itself. Days passed. 'When you look while recalling the names of what you see,' he thought, 'you're at best seeing to the limit of example. By casting off those names, you see further.' As Fain followed this thread of thought and realised that wisdom never comes of approval, he found that the landscape was tilting. Soon he was grasping the hand rope as the world, the bridge and himself turned entirely upside-down. Below his hanging head smoke rushed into the sky, and above his feet were caves of cremation from which golden holes breathed dirty steam.

As he stepped hesitantly forward it became clear that his vision had inverted, not the world. His eyeballs had revolved like two doorknobs, and it would take a while for his mind to straighten the world picture again. As Fain realised this, he saw a heat-blurred, haggard-looking figure walking toward him along the bridge. He braced his wits as they met.

'Are you the challenger with the five questions?' the stranger rasped.

'No. Aren't you?'

'No. Don't you have any questions to ask me?'

'How long have you been walking?'

'Three days. You?'

'Three, the same. So the bridge takes six days to cross and we're in the middle. Where do you think you're going?'

'The rainforest. Is that where you came from?'

'Yes. What's ahead of me?'

'The black desert and the dune cities. Do you have any advice for me?'

'If you want to enter the pyramid, flatter the eye. Anything I need to know?'

'Watch out for gnats.'

'Well, goodbye.'

'Goodbye.'

Now below his head was a landscape bleached and heavy as the calm after battle. It seemed to be several intermeshing labyrinths of ice, so tightly interlocked that none of them could function. As he walked past these pearlescent platforms the world continued to roll over, amid a torrent of pain. After several instants of flickering upright and coming loose again, the world picture finally anchored itself in place: sky above, ice below. It was like the skull of the world. 'Knowledge tells a story,' Fain thought, 'wisdom makes sense of it, power changes it.' Creeping sentinels of steam slowed over the scratched face of an iceberg. The silvered spars of gloom were like buildings under construction or in ruins. Again he glimpsed faces in sharded holes, and later a bloated hill made entirely of twitching hands. The creaking mineral hell became dirtier and darker until the bridge reached the opposite shore, and Fain stepped off onto a desert of black salt under a blue sky.

CHAPTER 16

In which Fain faces execution

After trudging through the desert for two days, Fain spotted a broad-backed animal with a flat head, near the gentle rise of a hill. Cart-sized and lizard-like, it was trolling along and looking cute as it inspected the ground. 'This thing looks pretty harmless,' Fain thought, and retrieved the rope from his pack. Looping this into a simple bit harness, he approached the quiet creature from behind and leapt onto its back, throwing the harness over its head so that it wedged between its jaws. The creature seemed startled but was soon conveying Fain across the jet salt plains.

He soon approached a walled city. The entrance was a keyhole two hundred feet high, without a door. Fain made his triumphal entry to find himself in a city foresquare. At its centre was a solid glass blue obelisk a hundred feet tall in which was suspended the body of an insect the size of a man, and around this thronged a colourful market with citizens selling snow, blue sugar, paradice, tamarinds, alligator pears and another fruit like the hardened teardrops of a giant. As these citizens turned to stare at Fain, he noticed that they were all giant lizards like the one he was riding. The entire square fell silent.

Fain awoke in pain, standing chained in some sort

of royal court. What he at first thought a gong nearby was in fact a massive coin bearing the form of a coiled lizard. Groggily he regarded the reptile which sat in the chunky golden throne before him. A web-throated official was reading from a scrolled decree. 'And for the heinous crime of harnessing and riding upon our Royal Sovereign as He strolled the Royal Garden, Fain the Sorcerer shall hereby be beheaded in the public square.'

Fain tried to jump several days back, but nothing happened. 'They put a special band around your neck,' a small voice quailed into his left ear. It was Hex, the gecko. 'You bragged of your gifts immediately, just before twenty-nine of these reptiles knocked you down and started breaking your bones. The band binds your powers. But they can't see me—tee hee!'

But when the guards roughly turned Fain to lead him away for execution, Hex sprang alarmed from his shoulder and landed on the arm of the King's throne, flushing through with the gold of his background. The King and his court gasped.

'Wait!' called the King, halting the guards. 'Remember Draak's prophecy!' He gestured with a paddle-like claw to the huge disc portraying a gold lizard whorled about itself. 'The Golden Salamander will bring transformation to our city!'

Fain immediately urged Hex to stay where he was.

For the next few days, Hex and Fain were treated like gods. Fain confirmed that Hex was the golden salamander, thankful that nobody could see he had not capitalised the remark. So long as Hex stayed on the throne he was safe. Freed from the binding ring, Fain had become friendly with the Lizard King and, accepting a grape from a scaly maiden, asked him the significance of the obelisk in the town square, the plinth beneath it bearing beneath the legend WHEN THE COWARD HAS CAUSE. 'We were once regularly besieged by the swarm-race of insects which dwell in the hive dunes to the east,' the King told him. 'But a sorcerer called Draak captured their King and suspended him in that obelisk. The blue glass is magicked in such a way that a cowardly scream of sufficient pitch would shatter it and release the Insect King. Look close at the city wall and you will see an insect lookout always observing the square. Through Draak's manoeuvre all is held in suspension. The insects are held in abeyance while we hold their king and might harm him. And we are held strong by the threat of the Insect King's release were we to fail in courage. There are still huge insects to the east that grow to resemble our children crucified, specifically to draw us close enough to snare and digest. They are creatures who know so little about their own motivations we have to fill it all in ourselves—but how does that help anything, if none of the thought processes we used to work it out, are happening in their minds when they do it? If it derives from incoherence?'

As a lizard maiden offered purple sugar on a hand like a lilypad, Fain expressed surprise that a race of giant lizards had any trouble defeating insects. 'We used to eat them en masse,' said the King, 'but gorged so much we couldn't stand those crunchy bastards any more. Our tongues, which were once whiplike and prehensile, have atrophied, look.' And he let his tongue dangle out like a rope.

'Still,' said Fain, 'you could squash them with those paddle-hands of yours—like *that*!'

And by way of demonstration he slapped his hand down on the throne's arm-rest, forgetting that the golden Hex crouched there. The lizard saved himself by springing away and landed on the ground, becoming instantly grey. Before he knew what was happening, Fain felt the magic-binding ring clamp around his neck again.

Five minutes later Fain was walking up some wooden steps to a platform in the city square. The executioner had an axe but didn't seem unhappy to see him. 'You'd better start killing me, headsman,' Fain squeaked, 'or I'll be asnore on the block. Credit the next neck?'

The green axeman ignored his bluff, roping Hex to the back of Fain's neck. He pushed Fain's face sideways against the rough, gravelly block so that Fain could see the lizard crowd and the King on a bier nearby.

'Imposter, even if we do not execute you,' the King called, 'uniformity and procedures will kill you, in a way.'

Hearing the axe-head zing as the executioner picked it up, Fain released the most cowardly scream to have been heard in centuries. The glass obelisk shattered, releasing the form trapped inside. Unblurred and unsupported, the insectile body collapsed and was something else. Its bug-eyed head was a washbasin, a couple of sieves and some bulrushes. Its many legs were branches. Its abdomen was a barrel tipped with a spike helmet and its wings were large fans stolen from the imperial palace. A sibilant cry of cheated rage thrilled from the insect lookout on the city wall.

A thundering vibrated through the hard-caked earth and, within moments, thousands of massive brown insects poured into the city like a river of swords.

Three minutes later Fain escaped into the desert, riding on the Lizard King.

CHAPTER 17

In which Fain enters a city of artificial creatures

Five days later they entered a city which seemed like a gigantic machine. Buildings of hammered bronze breathed like kettles and smelt of bonfires, and whale-like boats floated through the sky. A giant living arrowhead lumbered toward Fain on carved lion's feet. It was festooned with gold quincunxes and quatrefoils like a decorated general. Looking closer at this embroidered heavy ordnance, Fain was startled to see, behind a smoked glass panel in its belly, a spinning dice.

Nearby an old man dressed in an acid green harlequin uniform was busy with playing a trumpet, folding balloons and other street-emptying exploits. He was observing his own actions with apparent bafflement through smashed spectacles. His body bent like a bow, he feebly juggled silver rings and slapped them together without interest, interlinking them. Several metal people were watching his display. 'A vagabond in a crush hat eh?' said one of them.

'Do creatures like you enjoy these displays of buffoonery?' Fain asked the living wedge.

'These actions in the road are permitted, though for safety purposes we avoid understanding them.'

At that moment the prancing relic collapsed, dropping his three cups. Seeing that all three were empty, the artificial onlookers rumbled among themselves and wandered off. Fain loaded the old clown onto the Lizard King's back and they took him to what he whispered was his home, a hovel heated by wasps. Given a sip of wine, the jester roused enough to damn his circumstances. 'Those creatures outside, they are dicehearts, mechanical people, and this is Diceheart City.'

'I've seen a mechanical man before. Who made these?'

'Drake the Adept, in an access of power like a sneeze. So here they are, created and abandoned, with no idea of the why of any of it. So different than ourselves? It's very complicated, how I know this; and to understand it, you would have to become another person. No bad thing.'

'How did you get here?' asked the Lizard King, whose bulk filled most of the room.

'I sought Drake the Adept, but was already in a desperate condition when I arrived—entering the city, I merely tripped and smashed nosefirst on the ground. The incident caused the fastest assemblage of bastards I've ever seen. Some chugged, some wheezed, but none attempted an expression never done before. If there was a chance of that, oh I'd gladly damage my muzzle again, try and stop me. But the city controls even such feeble projects. They have their hierarchy. Only the upper echelons have pincers, for instance. However, they did pay. Since then I've tried year after year to find what amuses those contraptions, but to little avail. All I have learned are the divers arts of the cornered man: snarling, begging, screaming, sobbing, whispering, fainting, feinting, painting, panting, ranting and, of course, sitting down.'

'It sounds like being cornered is an education in itself.'

'And cheap. Remember that. But now, you take the stupid hat and bells of irritation—I am finished.'

'I don't want to be a jester!' Fain protested.

'You can use it,' whispered Hex, who had been removed to Fain's shoulder again.

'I won't be advised by a tile.'

'You need something,' said the old greybeard, 'and trick-magic is about misdirection. By concealing your desires, you may trick people into being cruel about the wrong thing.'

And with that, the jester expelled his vitality like a gas.

The Lizard King moved into the old clown's house, and Fain donned the scarf, cap and bells, setting out to annoy one and all in the street. He started to flourish a bit of velvet around, manipulating it as though about to produce something from thin air. A crowd of dicehearts began to gather. Fain continued to manipulate the velvet, looking increasingly desperate. After an hour of this, Fain was approached by a scuttling carapace constable the size of a horse. Eight spiderlike legs of bone conveyed a skeletal cage fronted by a titanic, yawping set of humanlike jaws. As it capered and tilted along, a song of illness choired from its hollows.

'The compropede will take you to be judged,' said an armorite with a head of metal thorns and eyes of cherry-coloured glass. 'You must be eaten into the cage.'

The jawed conveyance began to nip at Fain, who struggled as he was gathered horribly into the giant mouth and ejected into the cage on its back. Fain felt he was on the jolting cart to the gallows.

The Diceheart Palace was topped by two massive

milk-glass hands raised as if in prayer but slightly apart, and at such a height that Fain could only imagine he saw some fluctuation or effect between them. Fain was disgorged finally within a court of authority. At its head was what Fain took to be the diceheart autarch, a massive mechanical heart which unfolded like a rose to reveal a pearl the size of a cannonball. Flanking this on one side was an armorite with pincers and a head like a sky-blue minaret, and on the other a dull olive-coloured sarcophagus with eight legs, topped with a baby head of red studs. The walls were crowded with onlookers, or perhaps mere regulatory devices.

'They tell me you are king of this place,' Fain addressed the rose. 'Now I see their claim is rather farfetched.'

'Your dismal antics in the street have bored one and all,' tolled the rose, 'with your flourishes, time-wasting, and jewellery made from apricot stones.'

'Don't be confused by his accusations,' whispered Hex, 'it's his way of showing he's curious about you. He thinks he's asked a question and so expects a reply.'

Unaware of what question had been intended, Fain decided upon simple truth. 'I am Fain the Sorcerer, and I quite frankly hate it here. Empty metal creatures, your city is a marvel! I suppose its emulation of a lobster halved lengthwise is symbolic? A community of dolls, ministers and tin soldiers the shape of fat moths—what's the point?'

His audience looked at each other and began chugging strangely, jigging up and down.

'Indeed you are all so begging for a punch in the nozzle I cannot find it in my heart to disappoint you.'

The dicehearts were laughing, with a light squeak of hinges.

'I find you empty, and suspect that you are, technically, dead. This rack-and-pinion morality of yours, like yourselves, is large but as weightless as an owl. And it ejects blue smoke!'

There was amiable uproar in the court. What the old jester hadn't realised was that the dicehearts found truth amusing, their laughter a means to evade it. They were more closely modelled upon humanity than he had suspected.

Fain turned to a nearby observer, a round frame in which pink lace flubbered with every breeze. An eye occasionally opened in the membrane, then clenched away again.

'You sir—that rather fanciful assemblage which exists where your head should be—need any help getting rid of it? Observe as I juggle this cloud of dust!'

Fain gestured for quiet in the ensuing chatter and, approaching the autarch, announced: 'My main intention was to perform a very particular illusion for you, the upper echelons of the city. Observe these dozen large metal rings.' Fain clashed them together. 'I will perform a disappearance, with the aid of an assistant— you sir!' He led the pincered, minaret-headed courtier into the performance area, much to the apparent delight of all.

Fain slipped the rings together, linking them, then unlinked them and juggled with them, catching four on each arm and four around his neck.

'Now sir, use those pincers of yours to snip through the rings on my right arm.'

The diceheart sliced through them, the twanged tangle hitting the floor.

'And through the rings on my left.'

The diceheart cut through these.

Fain removed his scarf. 'And—careful now—those around my neck!'

The assistant snipped through the five rings about Fain's neck.

'And now I will disappear and steal the royal barge!'

Freed from the binding ring, Fain vanished and walked out of the hilarity-filled court. The airboats were docked beside the milk-glass palace. He re-appeared as he walked up the gangplank to one of the ballooned barges. A tall, white-haired man in a black robe was stood at the front tiller, and Fain was about to order him to cast off when the guy ropes writhed loose, the gangplank fell away and the ship pulled into the sky with frightening speed. The old jester turned from the tiller to look at Fain, then seemed to suck in a hard breath, his white beard retreating into his chin. He removed his smashed spectacles and the eyes told Fain that this was Drake the Adept.

CHAPTER 18

In which Fain studies with Drake the Adept

Drake's modest fortress was in the mountains to the north, its entrance concealed behind a waterfall. As he walked into the comfort of this sanctuary, Fain stopped short upon the deep emerald carpet. It reminded him of the sea around the mermaid's island. Why had he left?

Drake led him through into a wizard's laboratory hung with triangular clocks, and explained the principles of building a diceheart. 'Like many human beings, it owns only three opinions and, by alternating these to the right timing, it can reproduce the external appearance of thought.'

Fain inspected bone bottles full of glass dust, bandaged toys with beaks, rusted autumnal fruit studded with nails, fragments of black honeycomb, an Ace of Hearts fossilized like a trilobite, an oversized sandtimer clotted fast with blood, a black rose on dark green velvet, and a skull of expertly fitted ebony and rosewood. He remembered a treasure the mermaid had shown him, a salmon carved from pink quartz.

Here were cantraps on onion paper furry with age and books with sectioned spines like the spines of fossils. 'What happened to the Insect King?' he asked.

'He wished to escape the nonsense of war and I enabled him, leaving a replica in amber while he quietly absconded to a more pleasing and fruitful life. This is one of his volumes here.' Fain took the proffered book: *A Guide to Beekeeping*. 'What's this other one about? *The Seventy-Eighth Lie.*'

'The wise know of seventy-seven species of lie and can see them all quite clearly. I notice you're unable to lie at present.'

'My word is my bond. I have to travel forward in time to undo it.'

'You were fortunate to blunder upon time travel as your first gift. Do you see how your thin life has changed and grown richer? Time is central to life. Anything which is a process, requires the dimension of time. Flowers require it, for instance. Only something which is fixed and finished does not. Is it coincidental that when a thing is complete and fixed, as in a museum, all life goes out of it? You will know when someone has manipulated time because the day misses a beat.'

'The time idol Suvramizana told me that decisive moments can tell a lot about a man.'

'The formula of such a moment is rich and precise, like the deepest joke. Hackler Thorn too had one in particular that might be of interest to you. As a child, he encountered a monster—a werewolf, it seems. It walked in to his very nursery one night. Over the years, Thorn's defences froze to potency. His arms dream quite separate dreams from his head. Arm dreams. To do with odd structural choices, ivory, wood, and tipped liquid angles.'

'How do you know I'm searching for Thorn?'

'For the same reason I knew you were searching for me. You leave traces throughout time. I met you before we met. Be grateful that Thorn doesn't have that power.'

'You're immortal?'

'Amortal. We arrive with death in us like a watermark. Since a person can live only a certain number of years, why not travel back and forth through those years, back and forth, eternally? Say, seventy years, plus the entire surface of the world: not bad. But there may come a moment in a person's life when he finds that he has sampled finally all that is on life's menu—and upon considering the bill of fare, decides in all reason that it is a shabby, limited affair and not to his taste. I won't be around much longer.'

Drake indicated a globe hung with the countries and nations peculiar to it. Touching its surface, it cleared like glass and gutless wonders wraithed upon its surface. 'These are Vagues—thoughts to do large things, but without real intent. Something more than daydreams but far less than acted plans. Look how beautiful these kinds of cities are. A shame.'

'I move through life leaving blunders behind me like seeds to hatch a disastrous reputation—one I intend to be luxuriant and intricately interwoven.'

'Have you forgotten the Princess?'

Fain gasped. 'Yes, I had. And even now that you remind me, I can only remember her mouth. Whatever became of her?'

'Perhaps she's in trouble, perhaps merely bored. Or both.'

'Next time I meet the old man, I'll ask that all the gifts and powers I have, she must also have—then I'll think no more about her.'

'That's certainly a plan,' said Drake, walking away. 'After all, understanding flows backwards.'

Drake was as tall as the human bloodstream would allow, and taller, having a spare heart stowed in each shoulder. His sanctuary was a place of rose windows, the truth held inside a retort, and silver padlocks on every mirror. Behind the veil of water Fain studied for a year, learning to approach adversaries through their shadows, to read the code on the backs of Capricorn beetles, to transmute solid objects into water vapour, to carry an instantly accessible disguise by looking different from the side than from the front, to breathe backwards, to drink from veins in the earth, to fashion a sharrow - an arrow which can pin someone's shadow in place - and to banish westwallow, a sour trance-like disease of taking others' orders and years from your own life. He heard a music made of eight varieties of silence, drank delirium nectar, and read a book of stories which could be browsed forever, its blessing and curse being that the same story was never found twice. A flower like a book, a book like a padlock, a padlock like a metal heart, a heart like a mineral clock. 'And remember to close your eyes when you sneeze or your eyeballs'll fly out at a hundred miles an hour,' Drake added.

'I have something very particular to say to you,' said Drake finally one day, petting a snake banded black and yellow like a wasp. 'Seagulls forget soldiers. The present is stronger.'

'Your personality's lacy enigmas are doing my nut in, master.'

'I'm sorry. But objectivity will not tell all.'

'Why not?'

'It lacks emotion. Therefore it doesn't have all the information. We disagree on many things because we see them as they are. The emotional half has dried out in you, your brief happiness almost forgotten. You and Thorn are not so unalike. And I would not have you die having grown only one wing.'

'You're scaring me. What do you mean?'

'Our time together is done. I grant you this curse and blessing: the day you truly see yourself for the fool you are, your fondest wish will be granted.'

Drake unlocked a mirror, and Fain stepped through into Envashes forest. He travelled back to a time before his previous visits to the old man, and approached the cave.

CHAPTER 19

In which Fain is finally a man of his word

'My queen to your rook nine!' (or something like that) cried the crazy old man after Fain smashed the urn. 'This urn is enchanted, and it falls to you to receive its final three wishes!'

'So,' said Fain. 'Three wishes eh? Well, I wish to be able to travel instantly forward in time to any point in the future I choose, while retaining my clothing and baggage. Secondly, I want to know where Hackler Thorn is at any time. Thirdly, I wish to be able to transport instantly to any place in this world that I choose, when I choose to do so, while retaining my clothing and baggage.'

'You choose well, cloaked stranger,' cackled the old lunatic.

Buying a store of rope and canvas, Fain travelled a thousand years into the future, finding himself immediately surrounded by dicehearts. They sped around him, belching smoke behind them and honking with laughter. And looking closer, Fain saw that human beings were trapped within them all. They were compropede captives, being sped to judgement! Fain could barely breathe. He wished himself forward another fifty years and time clenched the three thousand teeth of silence. He was standing in a landscape of human

71

skeletons in papery snow. Broken towers crowded a gloomy horizon. He transported himself to the dragon's cave, and lit a torch. 'Next time I should state a wish to be able to see in the dark,' he thought. The creature's ribcage was clean and still in the dead cavern, its doglike skull sad in the flickering light. He wished fire upon the skeleton and it burned, then he extinguished the fire. Roping the corpse into the canvas, he encircled the neck with his arms and wished himself above, then wished himself more than a thousand years back in time. Then he wished himself near to Camovine town. He left the dragon beneath a tree and wished himself into town, buying a horse and cart. Riding back to the dragon, he loaded it into the cart and set off again.

Seeing the expected figure appear over nearby trees, he dismounted and walked to the leafy clearing where the crumpled youth lay screaming, having sustained one-hundred-and-eleven broken bones. Pulling up the hood on his cloak, he knelt over the young man, administering absentia draft and explaining all the while what he was doing.

Soon the younger Fain was riding beside him on the wooden seat of the cart. 'We approach the city of Camovine,' Fain told him. 'Beware the local autarch. He keeps a mirror by which you may travel far, and he would use it to evacuate the town if he could, but a gewgaw lives within, which eats down those who enter and spits them out like apple cores.'

'I'm hungry,' said the young Fain.

'If I'm hungry I pull up one of the earth's veins, slit it open and drink from it. What else do *you* do?'

'Kill a warthog.'

'Which of itself has drunk from the veins of the earth.'

'I should have said "try" to kill a warthog. They're hard to find, and even harder to catch. To kill, perhaps impossible. It's the same with bears.'

'I know it is.'

'So this earth vein business might not be such a crazy idea.'

'Not crazy at all. Just boring. Lacking adventure, and thus creating no stories. And because it creates no stories, it is a wisdom repeatedly lost and only by chance rediscovered. True wisdom is like that. Not spectacular. This is Camovine. I leave you here.'

Leaving the young man at the city gate, Fain rode to an inn and lodged there a while. Presently he fetched the cart from the stable and took it further into town, waiting near the palace until he spotted the scorched figure of his younger self walking in. He brought the cart up to the palace entrance, removed the canvas from the coiled and gruesome skeleton of the dragon, and walked away, hearing delight and commotion behind him.

'Finally,' he thought with relief, 'my word need no longer be my bond.'

CHAPTER 20

In which Fain tracks Hackler Thorn through time

'Sand dunes really took a climb,' the old man seemed to say after Fain released him from the urn. 'This urn is enchanted, and it falls to you to receive its final three wishes!'

'Three wishes you say?' Fain said thoughtfully. 'Well, I would like to be able to see great distances, clearly, by bringing only the image close to my visual perceptions as though I were looking through the most powerful telescope ever created.' Fain had inspected a telescope at Drake's sanctuary, and hoped that the old man would understand. 'Secondly, I wish to be able to see in the dark, and by this I do not mean to be able merely to see the darkness, but to see in the darkness as though it were illuminated, though without conflagration. Thirdly, I wish that the sorcerer Thorn shall never enter the kingdom of Envashes or be there by any means.' For Fain knew that this was the scene of Thorn's abductions of the Princess and his several strangulations at Fain's own hands.

'You choose well, young stranger,' cackled the old lunatic.

Fain travelled back in time and then a hundred miles distant. He stood in dry wasteland at the base of a thousand-foot-high palace. It was a slender white wedge, the sky above it shimmering like silk.

Entering through a round door, Fain found himself in what seemed to be an abandoned cottage. Murked, unreadable wall portraits tilted at him.

There were no rooms above the cottage, the palace spike a solid decoy. Knowing the tricks of warlocks, Fain upended the heavy kitchen table and pushed it inward—it was a door leading to a stone flight of spiral stairs. Descending, he emerged into a strange chamber. Fain felt afraid of this room which was decorated from floor to walls to ceiling like a chessboard. On a small round table stood a bowl arranged with black flowers and white berries. The room had the odour of valerian. Fain passed through this, opening a tall triangular door onto a vast hall of meat. The slurry floor gave way beneath him and he fell further into a puzzle palace of trick perspectives and cut diamond masonry which resulted in pain rooms, chambers which gave him a poison headache within moments of entering. Here was useless furniture made of precious stones glued with human blood, and dark bronze statues with irregular panels removed to display innards of spinel glass and iolite. The infinite scintillations of the carpet hooked his eye and made him almost forget his purpose.

Finally, descending a grand staircase carved from whalebone, Fain reached the centre of the Cathedral of Knots. A throne was set at the bottom of several such staircases like a tiny stage in an amphitheatre. Today, Thorn looked like a giant insect hung with cutlery. A pearlhandled claw glinted in uterine light and Thorn had cast a spell against Fain, which Fain solidified inches before it hit—a flower like an orange boil clattered to the floor.

When Thorn opened his jaws it drew taut the twelve

wires which were strung between them, and these he strummed and plucked with his complicated claws in lieu of speaking normally. 'You were not invited,' he said.

'I apologise,' Fain told him. 'What's the reason for all these boring staircases?'

'Invisibility traps. It's incredibly difficult for an invisible intruder to walk down stairs.'

'Is that so?' said Fain with interest. 'I suppose it's because even if they're not blind, they can't see where they're placing their own feet.'

'Quite so.'

'What's this building made of? Bacon?'

'Marble! And it's a palace!'

'This underworld of yours appears to have been carved from apricots. And your throne—some sort of sugar fondant?'

'Solid rose quartz.'

'Ah! '

'And now that you are assured my stronghold is inedible, see what trouble your so-called civilisation will give you if I turn your head translucent.'

'Do your worst, Thorn. I don't think they'll find more than a brain and hinges up there: all facts. I notice your mouth opens sideways.'

'I've noticed it too. An unfortunate side-effect of m'villainy.'

'Yes—what's that all about?'

'Decomposition has disguised the grandest betrayals these many years.'

'So, the king burns on his throne like a torch in its niche. And jade gryphons guarding gold? Sickly taste!'

'Your sentences have a hydrochloric structure to

'em. You assure me they do not conceal some glamour or cantrap?'

Fain found himself inside a block of ice, and set about conjuring heat as he observed the blurred entrance of a trapdoor servant, black dumb fire behind its eyes. It was a walking bat monster, its musculature like red cobwebs, such as Thorn would later employ en masse. Thorn had stood, advancing with stretched jaws. 'I am a sword polished with ashes.'

Fain transported himself into the cottage kitchen and another forty years into the past. Upending the table again and pushing through it, he made his way to the chess room and felt a flicker of bad sensation. Thorn was seated at the small white round table. Today he was a gaunt albino with a silver half-moon blade arcing from the back of his head like a rudder. Fain seated himself opposite, on a garden seat woven from white metal. On the table was a cut white ivory diamond the size of a duck egg, each facet engraved with the face of a different insect. The room was filled with the scent of headache trees and everythyme. There was no triangular door.

Fain had learned from the mermaid the million colours of water, none of which had a name. Looking at Hackler Thorn, he said, 'Your luck is grey.'

Thorn's face twitched like a cat's ear. 'At least you're honest.'

'Is that really the least? I seek the truth, when there isn't anything better to do. Which there never is, Lord Thorn.'

'"Lord Thorn,"' Thorn repeated, savouring the words. 'I like that.' Looking up, Fain saw a chandelier of black crystal which hung like a widow spider.

'This prejudice against skulls and shadow,' said

Thorn. 'Both are necessary aren't they?'

'Absolutely,' said Fain. He was glad to have one of his own arguments expressed.

'Life is quantum entanglement, a red labyrinth of delays and repeated perplexities. I was an innocent once, but now I'm reformed. And you, with that bog of shadows you call a mind. Who the hell are *you*?'

Fain saw Thorn's face prowing out, beginning to change, and instantly wished himself in the cottage kitchen. Above, he wished himself another fifty years back. The kitchen seemed quite orderly, the portraits of squires and maidens quite legible, and there were devices and pieces of meat on the table. Fain swept them off, upended the table and walked at it, breaking his nose. Staggering outside into a bright garden clogged with roses, he saw Thorn standing near a stone basin which tumbled a fountain of fresh water. Today Thorn was a skeleton full of meat and a head bound in human skin. Fain realised abruptly that this was Thorn simply presented as human. The warlock wore a black cloak decorated with triangular autumn leaves and red heart snails. He was bending to examine the earth. 'Oh yes nature trots out the dandelions, big deal.'

'Mr Thorn,' Fain called.

Thorn straightened up, frowning. 'Who are you? And my name's not Thorn.' He bent to examine a rose. 'Another tag of slithering formulae.' He stood, and kicked it from the earth.

'No sense in that,' said Fain. 'You may as well fight against your own gums.'

'Your nose is bleeding. And anyway, maybe I will. I happen to hate my gums, why not? Squatting there while I do all the work. It's bad enough I'm trapped in this skull and viewing the world through these crooked teeth. And look—the garden is filthy with petals!'

Fain laughed, and because he did not want to offend the man, who was standing directly in front of him, he laughed from both sides of his mouth while keeping the middle closed—the effect was apparently not what he'd hoped for, as the man looked suddenly startled and incredulous.

'I could arrange to have you bitten by a gnome,' the man told him.

'Not much fun.'

'Fun? When you inspire indignation you know you're alive.'

'I agree,' said Fain emphatically. 'Someone who loves the world cannot remain unstirred.'

The man seemed unconvinced. 'These verbal trinkets clink in your own wind. Let's sit over there, I'll explain something to you.'

Fain glanced back at the simple, towerless cottage as the man who would be Thorn led him to a terrace rich with broken capillaries. Here was the stone image of a wingless lion and the earthenware feet of a missing statue. A garden table bore a book bound in red leather. Tea stains made the yellowish tablecloth resemble the pelt of a giraffe. As they sat down, Fain perceived Thorn's heart perched like a bulbul in a calcium birdcage. Fain looked beyond him at the box-hedges, and behind a green metal gate, a garden of fountains and swans and cherry mint breezes. Here and there through the garden moved giant snails with the heads of crocodiles. The tile lizard was sunning itself, glued to Fain's shoulder.

'You are as suspect as surgeon water,' said the man, 'whoever you are. But I can cope with that. I was born with a head for my own personal use, and free will— of a kind. Take a gander at this.' He opened the book with a thump. 'If a book's not big enough to creak it's worthless to a professional scholar.'

'Does a truth require the death of so many trees to be stated once?'

'Listen to this: "Are they stars or holes in the trees? Are they truths or holes in the lies?"' Then he sat back, pleased with himself.

'I'm with you so far.'

'So far you idiot? I just explained the universe!'

'Most people *build* on the obvious to make a point. You seem to have run out of steam.'

'Steam is it? I'll kill you!' The man threw himself across the table at Fain, who vanished and reappeared near an ivy-twined pillar nearby.

'It's such a beautiful day—must we fight? I've looked forward to meeting you. I want to understand things. Did you write this book?'

'Of course not!'

'Then these are not your own thoughts. Tell me your own thoughts.' Fain gestured to a pair of skeletons hung by manacles from an overgrown wall. 'For instance, these fellows look a bit pasty. What's the story behind those?'

'Pasty? They're skeletons. Pastiness is the least of their concerns.'

'What's the greatest then?'

'Their lack of usefulness, I suppose. The people who ran them are gone—why must these remain?'

'Perhaps some creatures re-use such skeletons the way certain snails take up residence in the shells of their dead comrades.'

'Let us hope. Meanwhile, you may have noticed these giant snails with the heads of crocodiles.' The man led Fain into the larger garden. 'I call them Vetifers—though, like all animals, they do not respond. But will we as a people ever take the hint and stop putting names on animals? I don't think so.'

'They look quite cute. Are they dangerous?'

'They differ from crocodiles in that they are much, much faster.'

'But they're hardly moving.'

'Crocodiles spend most of their time completely motionless. Therefore these creatures, though moving very slowly, are much, much faster than crocodiles. Aren't you, Tony?'

The particular Vetifer which the man had turned to address lashed suddenly at him and he leapt back, laughing.

'Not such a laugh when you're chained to a floor staple. I keep these things to get me over a fear from childhood. Guess what happened to me.'

'Pounced upon by eight screaming chimps?'

'No!'

'Then I don't want to know,' said Fain, and realised too late that the man had been referring to the werewolf encounter of his infancy. Careful not to curse himself, Fain tried to veer the conversation back on track. 'However, childhood has always interested me. What of your parents?'

'Gone. And my servants are fish with training wheels—see?'

Fain looked to a pavilion at the far end of the garden, where indistinct devices moved in circles. 'Alright.'

'Tiny bells line their stomachs to alarm upon escape. I envy them—they grew with no illusions of safety or protection.'

'We have not been introduced, sir—I am Fain the Gardener.'

'Geoffrey Cubeline.'

'How long have you lived here, Mr Cubeline?'

'Thirty-eight years,' said Cubeline. 'All my life.'

'I'm sorry, Mr Cubeline,' said Fain, and travelled twenty years into the past. He stood in the midst of trees. Returning to the terrace, he entered a black cloud of flies which feasted around the bodies of a man and woman who hung chained from a wall, their bellies bursted open in a now dry tumble of black complication.

Approaching the cottage through the small garden, Fain was startled when the door opened and a young man stepped out with a look of such poison sadness the taste of bile came up in Fain's mouth and he wished himself ten years back. He stood in the garden hearing the silence of a child, the sound of a family. He took himself back into the night and entered the cottage invisibly, reappearing to pick his way through the darkness. Remembering his new ability to see in the dark, he invoked this as he entered the room of the child who would be Thorn. What happened here on this night?

The child let out a choked gasp and began to scream. Startled, Fain looked around himself and saw a long mouth in a mirror. It was his own mouth. In order to see in the dark, he had become a giant wolf.

CHAPTER 21

In which Fain tries to help

Fain returned to his own time but had no immediate desire to revisit the crazy old man at the cave. And he was so disturbed by his glimpses of the future that he rarely used that gift again, and sometimes felt a creeping horror when he remembered the insidious forward motion of time which seemed the natural condition. He would later wonder if, since he had the choice, he might set up his life at an earlier time than that into which he had been born. Perhaps at a time when matters were less complicated. With his creeping bent for mermaid reflection, he could no longer abide to eat his magic sardines. He thought of the green gold grotto where the mermaid collected shells as though they were pirate treasure, and pirate treasure as though it were shells. Above all he wished for a place without blame.

For now, chastened by his faults, he travelled, attempting good deeds and observing the lay of things. He sauntered through the tatty wreck of a battlefield where birds, dogs and worms would suffer no interruption to their meal. He conversed on music with a huge black toad like a leather sack. He observed the chaos around a royal crier hailing the official declaration that all was well as the earth cracked and lava wrinkled toward him. He saw an elephantine monster stamp on a man so hard it left something in the mud resembling a Persian carpet, which a merchant then sold as such. He saw sails of shark fabric, vintage consolation swelling in vineyards and skulls tumbling in silt like conches. He climbed to the summit of a temple that was like a city of many levels, its walls covered with maps and diagrams of heaven. He saw stone idols eroded to facelessness and bound with vines, a dead hero's sword embedded in scarred fields, the stars grinding across the sky, foreign marble sunken in hot dirt, tyrants spooning cinders from children's mouths, populations credulous and bovine, and kings with minds the consistency of bread. He visited a land where snow was cinnamon-flavoured for a reason everyone was too guilt-laced to reveal, and a civilisation of honest fear in which people gibbered in cages while lions prowled free. He battled and befriended a giant worm with a vortex for a mouth, and played cards with the Great White Kings of Hell. He travelled twice more through the mirror of Camovine, freeing Glut. He saw knights slugging it out in a pine-pinned clearing for ideas that were not their own. He walked through an empire of warring statues, saw the truth carved into beeswax and eaten, and moths full of gold-dust. On sunned ruins vagabonds sat exalted and with eyes closed.

One day Fain followed a trail of trees into a village. 'Welcome to Joisy,' hailed a young man who was striding away from him. 'You are welcome in my home.' The man set about winding a bucket of water from a well.

'Thank you,' said Fain. 'Where is your home?'

'I'll take you there,' said the man and withdrew the bucket, walking toward a small house. Then he suddenly wheeled about, dropped the bucket and ran off the opposite way, leaving Fain briefly startled but, knowing humanity for what it was, barely wondering. Fain picked up the bucket and entered the house, which he discovered to be adequately furnished but without a roof. Nor was there any wall above any of the doors. Presently the young man entered, smiling. 'Make yourself at home. I am Tagore.'

Tagore swerved aside and batted against the wall, then seemed to calm down and prepared a meal for which Fain was grateful. When Fain sat down to eat, however, Tagore stood nervously, apparently awaiting some signal that he could be seated. 'Won't you join me?' Fain asked.

A woman barrelled into the house and slammed against the table, sitting down opposite Fain. Fain could see a tangle of wires above her head.

'This is my wife, Vellum.'

'Welcome. It seems Tagore will not be sitting with us this evening. He'll probably have to sleep standing up.'

'You're puppets,' said Fain. 'Made of meat.'

'We're people, like you,' said Tagore. 'But with these things attached.' Tagore drew a finger down one of the almost invisible wires projecting upward from his head. He did this as though the wire were the edge of a blade. Fain followed the wires upward with his eye, until he was looking at a sky full of clouds. Tagore continued: 'You'll find most people here deny it, deny they have no roof, and never look up. They deal with their powerlessness by pretending it's not the case.'

'While we believe that, since we're powerless, why deny the truth of it?' said Vellum brightly.

Fain threw his sight beyond the clouds and was there as incognito eyes. Hundreds of teal blue dragons wheeled crowing in a dazzling chill. He blinked and shook his head.

'We made the wires too strong to cut,' Tagore was saying.

'*You* made them?'

'Hundreds of years ago,' Vellum explained, 'we were preyed upon by dragons. Finally, the townspeople lassoed the dragons' legs in order to control the creatures and thus retain our sovereignty, freedom and independence. It was our grand experiment. The wires were the precise length to add weight to the affair and thus hamper and tire the monsters. Any attack by the dragons, dipping below full height, was forewarned by a slackening in the wires. But the creatures, being on high, unobserved, and given full means, now control the people. The change was stealthy as dust and still denied. And the wires are now too entangled around the people and around the dragons' talons to ever disentangle, until a person dies and rots away. Then their wires are taken up in fear by a son or daughter. The warning slack in the wires is useless, as we have no shelter.'

'In any case,' added Tagore, 'they can take us wherever they want for the attack. One of us will simply be walked out of the village into the wasteland, and never come back.'

'My dragon is gliding a little low,' said Vellum, standing. 'I'll take him to see.'

Vellum took Fain into the wasteland outside the village. Here she showed him ribbons of clothes on a hutch of sticky bones. Some of the bones were suspended a few feet off the ground, turning on a wire like a weathervane. The wires proceeded into the sky.

'Hasn't anyone ever rebelled?' he asked.

'Occasionally someone will try to pull the strings or make themselves sluggish and unmoveable. Most townspeople call it "getting heavy". It's frowned upon because it reminds us of our situation.' Vellum stopped talking abruptly—her wires were gathering and clouding around her shoulders like thread feeding from a loom. As she looked up a dragon swooped down at her, tearing off her head and spitting it into the grass. The monster settled upon the body, bit into it and set about pulling a necklace of meat from the wound.

Recovering from his shock, Fain materialised at a point which overlapped with the dragon, blasting it aside. He had destroyed his own right arm and blown a hole in the dragon's belly, from which garlands of gore were spurting. Fain straddled the dragon. 'Agree not to attack these idiots! Then you can work together to untangle and unattach the strings.'

'It's our nature to attack,' rasped the dragon, 'and if possible, herd people. These wires give us a direct line to our victims—we know exactly where to find them, whether for a kill or one in a long series of snacks. And in the meantime, controlling their affairs is amusing. We have good hearing. We know if they discuss rebellion. We use what we are given.'

Fain set fire to the dragon, sealed his shoulder with a scab of black glass and returned to the village. Tagore, in grief and fury, agreed to call the villagers together at the well.

Fain whispered: 'You are all aware that these silvery facsimiles of freedom are actually chains. There are several ways to change this situation. Take hold of large rocks and leap into the bottomless chasm near here, dragging down a dragon with you to their death and yours. Entangle your wires in the winch drum above this well, and wind your dragon down from the sky. Or allow me, Fain the Sorcerer, to change everything, either by appearing in the sky and summoning fire upon the dragons, or travelling back in time to prevent this situation from beginning.'

Fain expected a debate on the possibilities of each plan: that the chasm option was rash, that the well option could work only one dragon at a time, leaving everyone else open to attack. But in the faces around him he saw no fear: only embarrassment, evasion, or anger directed at him. While refusing him permission to interfere with their problem, they stated it vaguely enough to allow that there was no problem to be solved.

As Fain took his leave of the village, Tagore bid him farewell. Tagore seemed ashamed for his fellow villagers, but Fain was proud that this one man planned to drag his dragon from the sky, one way or another. He hugged him warmly, and walked away.

Stymied and exhausted, Fain decided his travels were over.

CHAPTER 22

In which Fain encounters a witch

His head freed from the urn, the old man said 'Ham is really put in wine?' or something like that, and added 'This urn is enchanted, and it falls to you to receive its final three wishes!'

'Three wishes eh?' Fain said thoughtfully. He could not berate the old man without giving away the fact that he had had wishes from him before. He proceeded with his list. 'Well, I wish to have the power to effortlessly and instantly make manifest in my immediate vicinity any object I desire, free to my ownership. Secondly, I wish to be able to shapeshift into the shape of any object or animal I wish to, and back again, when I wish to, to my own human form, without dissembling my innards or otherwise wrecking my health. Thirdly, I want to be able to fly, by merely wishing to do so, while retaining my clothing and luggage, without means of a device, and by this I mean the ability to fly upward and also horizontally and at any other angle I choose, at any speed I choose, and not merely falling downward.'

'You choose well, young stranger,' cackled the old lunatic. Fain walked away, went back in time an hour, walked back and helped the old man's head out of the urn. 'Can you really butcher rhyme?' said the man, or something like that, and then told Fain about the three wishes.

'Only three wishes? Well, I happen to be able to see at great distances as though through the strongest telescope ever created, but observing conversations and certain other scenes in this way can be frustrating, and so I wish to be able to hear at great distances, only at times when I want this power to manifest. Secondly, that the sardines I can currently draw magically from my pockets should instead be replaced by chestnuts. Thirdly, I wish that all my magical powers should be imparted to Princess Aleksa of Envashes, while yet retaining such powers myself.'

'You choose well, young stranger,' cackled the codger.

Fain transported himself to a warmer continent and over the next several years raised a blue jade palace beside a blue river. Economy was gone from sight the minute the golden pipes took hold. He gathered knowledge and power objects to equal those of Drake's sanctuary. He sat in a floating seat like a huge halfnut surrounded by crystal skulls, magic lamps and shrike mirrors, dealing glass tarot onto thin space. Hex, having absorbed all of Drake's lessons, finally managed to assume his own colour, while retaining the option to blend in. The palace weathered an occasional warm monsoon, Fain taking tea on a jade patio projecting into white air.

In the one hundredth year of his rule Fain came to hear of a powerful sorceress named Pernicia who was in the habit of making people into statues with a casual switch of her hand. After another two years the witch rode out of a purple-stained sky on a canary-yellow lash dragon. As this clasped to a stop on the landing stage of the main library, Fain looked up from his seat at the fireplace. He was now a white-haired, sleek-headed vulture of a man with mild eyes. 'The Princess looks amazing,' he thought. 'Off-course beauty is the wildest.'

'Allow me to finish this chapter,' he said, returning to his book as the witch dismounted. 'You should read this: *The Adventures of Young Fade*. It's very good.'

Pernicia was removing her gloves and gazing about at the veins of brilliant metal in the library wall. 'In hard times good health is retained by safety or daring. You seem to have chosen safety, old man.'

'You're beautiful.'

'This body is a shell.'

'Some shells are beautiful, don't you think?' And Fain found himself thinking of the sea off the mermaid beach, tiny transparent creatures living like a tangle of ghosts. A thousands drinking mouths and red pulsing jellyfish like free hearts.

'Well, I'm human only in broad outline now, I'm glad to say. I suppose I should thank you before I kill you.'

'Has it been that bad?'

'Over a century ago I was the simple Princess of Envashes, when suddenly every idle wish I had became manifest. My nurse burst into flames, I found myself transported to the time of my childhood, I flew through the clouds, terrified. I was condemned as a witch, and so I was. I sought out Drake the Adept, but he evaded me. I was forced to seek out Hackler Thorn.'

'How *is* Geoffrey?'

'*Geoffrey?* Hackler is well, if a little confused these days. His memories keep changing. But he taught me. He helped me discover who was responsible for these powers. In the quest for my own power I have subjected myself to every inconvenience known to man or woman. I have felt pure might. As I entered rooms, you could hear god's teeth chattering.'

'Sounds reasonable. And yet here you are in foreign pants and bleating like an angry child.'

'It's as though all my rages are happening at once. I remember you but I don't remember you. We once met at the centre of a bridge, going opposite ways.'

'Really? I suppose an extreme demand faces its twin brother in the extreme position of reality.'

'Soon traces of greatness were dissolving in my hands as I discovered the truth.'

'That, being a force of nature, sorcery has no more doubt or answers than a flame.'

'Light doesn't preach,' Pernicia agreed. 'Nor does darkness, nor anything between the two. However, it has glamour. The steps between miracles are never referred to, but style is always allowed to remain. It will have to be enough.'

'Not for me.'

Pernicia stood behind his chair. 'Look at you, so strong and wrong. Salt of the earth.'

'I've striven to fail, but ...' Fain looked apologetic.

'Your corpse will have a small brook going through it before anyone realises you're dead.'

'People have been promising me terrifying consequences for years, and all I get is the same dross.'

'So how would you want it. Would you be turned to a statue, ivy clasped about your naked vitals?'

'The notion is strangely exciting.'

Pernicia switched the glass of the window to stone so that the place was blotted in darkness, the dragon locked outside. Only the firelight illuminated Fain's book.

'Now all the strange terrors of my travels seem unreal,' muttered Fain, looking into the flames. 'Even boring.'

Then he remembered the book.

'Ah, I'm almost done. Young Fade finds he must steal a red egg from a gryphon nest atop a mountain—he magics himself directly there, but finds himself inside the egg, surrounded by black jelly. Upon his breaking out, the gryphon thinks he is her chick. He is still in a stupor when she feeds him something terrible, and then pushes him off the mountain edge to teach him to fly. How will he survive such a fall?'

'I know a spell,' Pernicia whispered, 'that rids you of all your magic powers but the first you acquired.'

'Ah, the Sultan's Depth Spell. I know of it.'

She leaned down. Her kiss left him in astonishment.

'You just received it.'

'What.'

Pernicia stepped back, triumphant. 'Try it. Anything.'

Fain stood, unsteadily. He wished himself invisible, and remained visible. He wished a cage around Pernicia, and there was no cage.

Only his first gift.

But what of his last gift? Fain remembered the wording of his request, and the old man's perversity. 'That all my magical powers should be imparted to Princess Aleksa of Envashes, while yet retaining such powers myself.' He repeated to himself: 'While yet retaining such powers myself.'

'What?'

'You'll find you've lost all your own gifts, Pernicia, since you received them all at once, and you retain yours only while I yet retain mine.'

'The spell has loosened your wits.'

'You still have your dragon. And I still have one gift. Goodbye.'

Fain travelled fifty years back, spent a few weeks

gathering what he needed from the palace, left Hex in charge, went back another sixty or so years, and began the long journey to Envashes.

CHAPTER 23

In which Fain finds the old man

More than a year later, Fain arrived to find the mossed cave empty. With no way of knowing when the old lunatic would show up or of hastening time forward, Fain set up camp in the cave, and waited.

Over time, the few artefacts he had brought from the palace began to look strange on the shelves of the cave. Did they really belong in a palace? And how did *The Adventures of Young Fade* end? He sat inventing endings for the book. But wasn't the end already written?

Fain remembered a long golden beach, and shells of red gold collected in a green gold grotto. He remembered a woman with gold eyes and a hard smooth head like a seal's. Who was he waiting for?

He roasted chestnuts on a fire outside the cave, and those he didn't eat he stored in a jar. One night he tipped the jar over, hearing a nut rattling around inside which refused to fall out. Sticking his head inside, he quickly understood that he was stuck. He could smash the jar on the cave wall, but wasn't it valuable or special? He should wait a while before doing anything rash.

The next day he heard someone approaching the cave. It was a young man, sounding weary, and Fain remembered.

'Hello old lunatic. Let me help you with that.'

The young man smashed the urn from his head.

'Man, you really took your time,' said Fain, chuckling at the sight of his younger self, and told him about the three wishes.

'Only three wishes?' said his younger self. 'Well, I happen to be able to see at great distances as though through the strongest telescope ever created, but observing conversations and certain other scenes in this way can be frustrating, and so I wish to be able to hear at great distances, only at times when I want this power to manifest. Secondly, that the sardines I can currently draw magically from my pockets should instead be replaced by chestnuts. Thirdly, I wish that all my magical powers should be imparted to Princess Aleksa of Envashes, while yet retaining such powers myself.'

'You choose hell, young stranger,' Fain cackled. And he found himself traversing a golden mapless land via Drake's curse and blessing to arrive in the shallow surf of a warm beach. Beside him lay the mermaid, telling him about a conch shell through which he could speak into the dreams of any person anywhere.

No, he would not use the shell to escape paradise. He would be witness to the blue sky, and the flashing tail of his beloved. He would finish his lessons in understanding the ocean's sand-messages. He would live out his life where the sea polished every shell to a precious gem and colours lived for their own deep sake.